"You ruined my mother's career!"

Jo stared bitterly into the rugged, once-loved face, and hatred flowed through her like an electric current. Nick sat watching her in silence, with an odd curiosity.

"Don't you think you should know all the facts before you start throwing accusations like that around?" he asked finally.

"Can you deny it? You fired Emma to put your girlfriend in her place!" To her disgust, he responded with a bark of hard cold laughter.

"Oh, grow up, Jo. And save all this fury for the camera—I don't want any of your adolescent tantrums on the set. Do you understand?"

She didn't bother to answer. In a single stride she was out of the room, slamming the door behind her.

WELCOME
TO THE WONDERFUL WORLD
OF *Harlequin Romances*

Interesting, informative and entertaining,
each Harlequin Romance portrays an appealing
and original love story. With a varied array
of settings, we may lure you on an African safari,
to a quaint Welsh village, or an exotic Riviera
location—anywhere and everywhere that adventurous
men and women fall in love.

As publishers of Harlequin Romances, we're
extremely proud of our books. Since 1949,
Harlequin Enterprises has built its publishing
reputation on the solid base of quality and
originality. Our stories are the most popular
paperback romances sold in North America; every
month, six new titles are released and sold at
nearly every book-selling store in Canada and the
United States.

A free catalog listing all Harlequin Romances
can be yours by writing to the

HARLEQUIN READER SERVICE,
(In the U.S.) P.O. Box 52040, Phoenix, AZ 85072-2040
(In Canada) P.O. Box 2800, Postal Station A
5170 Yonge Street, Willowdale, Ont. M2N 5T5

We sincerely hope you enjoy reading
this Harlequin Romance.

Yours truly,

THE PUBLISHERS
Harlequin Romances

Once More with Feeling

Natalie Spark

Harlequin Books

TORONTO • NEW YORK • LONDON
AMSTERDAM • PARIS • SYDNEY • HAMBURG
STOCKHOLM • ATHENS • TOKYO • MILAN

Original hardcover edition published in 1984
by Mills & Boon Limited

ISBN 0-373-02633-1

Harlequin Romance first edition July 1984

CHAPTER ONE

'JOSEPHINE Montague!' Madge announced in her most unyielding Scottish accent. 'It's past nine o'clock and you'd better get up. I shall not answer any more telephone calls for you!'

Jo opened her eyes and allowed herself a second to surface from deep sleep into the reality of her familiar bedroom and the dour cosiness of Madge, the Montague housekeeper. 'Nine o'clock?' she repeated drowsily, and then sat up, alerted by her own words. 'Good God, Madge. Why didn't you wake me up before? I'll be late for school!'

'No, you won't,' the stout woman retorted. 'You have no school today. Only a matinée performance and you don't have to be there before three. And I didn't wake you up earlier because you went to bed at dawn. That's what you wrote in the note you left for me in the kitchen.'

'Oh, yes, of course,' Jo relaxed back against her cushions to wallow for a few more seconds in the memory of last night's triumph. 'Did you enjoy the show, Madge?' she asked, anticipating the grudging answer.

'It was all right, I reckon, for a drama school production.' A slight smile transformed the harsh, middle-aged face. 'But you, Josephine, you were good. For a few moments I even thought you were almost as good as your mother.'

'Did you really?'

The play they were referring to was Jo's first performance before an outside audience. After two years at the London Drama Academy, she had at last been considered worthy of carrying the leading role of Saint Joan in her academy's final-term production and, judging by the applause and the head-turning compliments showered on her at the party afterwards, her performance had been a hit.

'I did,' Madge reaffirmed drily. 'And don't you go fishing for more compliments, my girl. Up you get now! I've been pestered by phone calls for you from the moment I arrived this morning. And I have other chores to attend to beside playing social secretary to the young Miss Montague.'

As if to corroborate her statement, the phone started ringing again, its shrill sound jarring the blissful tranquillity of the large Hampstead house. 'There it goes again. Now, you answer it, Jo. I'll have tea ready for you in the kitchen.'

Jo swung her long legs out of bed and ran to the hall phone, her slim body buried under a huge masculine T-shirt which had always been her idea of night gear. She was a tall girl, and the well-toned muscles of her thighs and legs indicated long years of ballet practice and athletic activity. Yet the general impression was of porcelain fragility, enhanced by the serene beauty of a madonna-like face, long luxurious waves of honey-coloured hair and transparent creamy complexion. Only the large golden-brown eyes and the delicate yet firm mouth hinted at the determined and stubborn nature lurking behind the deceptively fragile, serene façade.

'Hello?' she said as she picked up the phone, her voice still a little husky with sleep.

'At last!' muttered a dry, masculine voice. 'Will you kindly instruct that Scots housekeeper of yours that next time I call, she's to wake you up immediately. This is my third call, you know.'

'I'm sorry,' Jo answered calmly. 'But I did go to bed very late and—'

'Don't whine!' the voice lectured, impatiently. 'If you can't take late nights you shouldn't have opted for an acting career.'

Jo remained unruffled. She was used to eccentric phone calls of this kind. It was one of the penalties one had to pay for being the daughter of a famous and popular actress like Emma Montague. 'I wasn't complaining,' she answered patiently. 'I was only explaining. Who are you, by the way?'

The pause indicated a mild amazement. 'Michael Staller, of course. Don't you recognise my voice?'

The name tore the last threads of sleep. Jo became tinglingly awake. Like every other hopeful drama school student, she had been hoping that one day she would be represented by the Staller Actors' Agency. Michael Staller was the most powerful and hence the most exclusive film and TV agent in London.

'Are you still there?' the voice snapped angrily.

'Oh, yes, Mr Staller, I'm here.' Jo tried to curb the rising excitement. 'But I think you got the wrong person. You probably want to talk to my mother. I'm Jo, not Emma Montague.'

'Don't be a fool, girl,' the man barked, exasperated. 'I know you're Jo. No one has Emma Montague's brown velvet voice. It's you I wanted to speak to.'

'Oh—' Jo was stunned. Michael Staller had been her mother's agent for over twenty years and naturally he and Jo had to meet occasionally. But the agent had always dismissed her as a likeable but definitely super-fluous appendix to the famous and lucrative Emma Montague. 'I see,' she finally broke the awkward silence.

'Good. Now, how soon can you be ready?'

'Ready for what?'

'I want you down in Knightsbridge in half an hour.'

Jo gasped. 'In half an hour? I couldn't get from Hampstead to Knightsbridge in half an hour even if I didn't bother to dress! I just got out of bed, Mr Staller . . .' she reminded the irate agent.

'Cut out the "Mr" bit, my dear. I prefer to be addressed by my name—Michael.'

'Yes, Michael . . .' Jo corrected herself, taken aback by her own composure. 'But it's rather awkward, you see. I have a matinée performance at the Drama Academy and I like to be there at least an hour before we go on . . .'

'You're not expected there before three-thirty—I've already checked it out with your teacher. So don't argue with me.'

Once again Jo needed a moment to collect her thoughts. Michael Staller had actually taken the trouble to call her school and find out whether she was free to meet him. It almost seemed as if she hadn't been awakened at all, and that last night's triumphant success and this phone call from a great agent were just a part of a recurrent pipe-dream.

'Traffic allowing, I might manage to get there by ten-thirty,' she said finally. 'Is that all right?'

'It's not, but I guess it'll have to do,' the voice snapped irritably. 'And don't come in your night gear either . . . I don't think they'd appreciate that.'

'They? Who's "They"?'

'The people you're going to audition for.'

This time, with the best will in the world, Jo couldn't maintain her cool manner. 'Audition? I'm having an audition?'

'Oh, didn't I mention that?' the agent was perfectly aware that he hadn't. 'Yes, an audition. They want you in the office at eleven sharp, so don't waste your time and mine over the phone.'

'Wait!' Jo cried before the phone went dead, on her. 'Can't you just tell me something about it? I mean, is it a play? TV?' There was a teasing silence on the other end. 'A film?' she whispered, awed.

'Something of the kind . . .'

'But—' desperately, she tried to remember what her mother had been telling her about auditions, 'don't I need to dress for the part? What kind of a character am I being auditioned for?'

Michael Staller's voice warmed unexpectedly: 'You've certainly picked up some professional know-how, girl. Quite right, of course. I should have thought of it myself . . .' There was a thinking pause. 'Tell you what: They want you looking young, very young. So just wear your usual student gear . . . and for God's sake,' he paused for a second, 'whatever you do, don't put any make-up on . . . You looked hideous last night. Don't they teach you to apply make-up properly in that posh academy of yours?'

Jo could hardly believe her ears. Every drama student had been trying to get Michael Staller to come and see his or her final-year performance, hoping he would deem them worthy of joining the illustrious list of his actors. Very few had managed, and those who did invariably found themselves on the narrow if not very straight path to stardom within a year. 'You mean, you saw me last night? You came to see the play?'

'I came to see *you*,' the agent specified, acknowledging the wonder in Jo's voice. 'I wouldn't risk my reputation recommending you without making sure you're any good, would I? The fact that you're your mother's daughter doesn't automatically make you a good actress, you know. See you in my office at ten-thirty, then.' Typically, he took it for granted that everybody knew where his office was. 'Don't be late.'

The dry voice was replaced by the irritating burr of the dead line. In a daze, Jo put down the receiver and stood there, her thoughts churning madly. An audition! A truly professional audition! And for a film, no less. Not yet out of drama school and already thrown into the arena!

'Mum,' she shrieked, crossing the hall and bursting into her mother's bedroom, 'you'll never guess what's just happened.'

Her thrilled shout fell flat, drawing no sleepy 'brown velvet' response. Instead she was greeted by a sunny but empty room and a huge undisturbed bed which gaped blankly back at her, mocking her excited outburst and instantly deflating the glowing cloud of triumph.

The heady exhilaration was gone, bringing back the angry anxiety which had been gnawing at her ever since her mother had walked out on her without a word of explanation or warning. Even after four weeks, Jo still woke up in the morning eager to share yesterday's events and today's plans over a first cup of morning tea with her mother, only to face again and again the hollow empty room.

'Madge,' she called down from the top of stairs, 'any letters from Emma this morning?'

'No letters,' Madge shouted back. 'Only a postcard. Shall I read it out for you?'

'No, I'll be down in a minute. Does it say anything new?'

'The usual . . . she sounds just fine.'

Her frustration somewhat alleviated by another sign of life from her mother, Jo returned to her own bedroom and automatically began to apply herself to the task of making herself presentable: a cool, self-possessed actress, preparing for the ordeal of a first professional audition. The golden haze of a dream-come-true had been deflated, nevertheless.

It wasn't living alone which depressed her; she was used to that. Emma was a wonderful, supportive mother and a great friend, but her life had always been ruled by the demands of her career which kept her filming for months on end in remote parts of the world. Jo, even as a child, had learnt to accept this state of affairs. Madge, whom she had known since early childhood, had always taken good care of her, and Emma's loving warmth and attentive attitude when at home had always been ample compensation for the long periods of absence. Yet loneliness was always lurking below the surface.

It hadn't always been like that. Jo sighed now as her eyes sought the large photograph of her father, smiling wryly down at her with a well-remembered affectionate amusement. She was never alone when Robert Montague was alive. He very rarely left London, too busy churning out his plays and film scripts. And even when he was shut away in the study, she was always comforted by the endless angry rattle of his old, much abused typewriter. He was always there when she needed him, no matter how busy and absorbed he was.

But Robert had been dead now for six years, and the hollow gaping ache he had left never healed. With him gone, Emma was forced to send her thirteen-year-old daughter to a boarding school and the cosy comfort of Jo's old home had been replaced by the competitive whirl of an exclusive Brighton girls' school. Only the holidays brought a sample of the old security. Emma never allowed her work to interfere with the precious weeks of Christmas and with the summer holidays which she jealously kept free and uninterrupted for Jo.

And, as Jo reluctantly had to remind herself, Nick Hayward was there also to relieve the ache of loneliness. For a while, he even managed to fill the gap left by the death of Robert Montague . . . until he too had deserted her.

Nevertheless, when Jo finished school and came back to London to start her strenuous training at the drama academy, her relationship with Emma deepened and strengthened now that they had mutual interests and ambitions. At nineteen, Jo was independent and mature enough to take her mother's filming commitments and lengthy absences as a matter of course.

But this time it was different.

Emma hadn't gone filming—quite the contrary. She had run away to hide her misery and disillusionment, unable to face the world after the disgraceful blow to her career and reputation as one of England's most celebrated stars. It was hard to think of Emma Montague, usually so courageous and confident, skulking away, but

Jo had no doubt that skulking was what she was doing, for she kept her whereabouts secret even from her own daughter.

It was this secrecy which had hurt Jo the most: the fact that her mother hadn't considered her mature enough to share her unhappiness. Emma wrote often enough, almost daily, assuring Jo of her good health and well-being, but refused to mention the reason for her sudden retirement nor allow Jo to come and be with her. 'I want to be alone,' she had written in her usual wry humour, quoting the famous Garbo line, 'so just stop worrying about me, love. I'm fine and having a blissful rest.'

To make matters worse, Emma wouldn't give Jo an address to write to. 'You can write to me or contact me in the case of an emergency through Nick Hayward,' she specified.

Nick Hayward.

Jo stopped brushing her long, thick honey-coloured hair and stared unseeingly at her reflection in the dressing-table mirror. The serene face betrayed nothing of the wave of red-hot rage that flooded her as that hateful name rose to the surface. With a shudder of irrepressible fury she saw the handsome, rugged face under its mop of thick, sun-bleached hair, and the crooked smile mocking her anger and humiliation with its uncaring, dismissive amusement.

For a moment, she forgot her anxiety for her mother, and sat there quivering with indignation, her gripping fingers punishing the inanimate brush.

How could her mother choose Nick Hayward as her only contact with the outside world, preferring him to her daughter, her numerous loyal friends, her agent?

Where was her pride, her usual cool-headed sense? How could she put her trust in that ruthlessly ambitious film director who had betrayed her so callously? For Jo had no doubt that it was he, trusted friend, who had been responsible for Emma's disgrace.

His betrayal didn't surprise her, for she herself had been a victim to it. She probably wouldn't have reacted with such gullible vehemence to the cheap sensational item in the gossip columns had it not been for the burden of bewildered, humiliated pain which she had been carrying silently within her for three long years and which had turned Nick Hayward, whom she had always loved and trusted into a feared, enigmatic stranger.

Jo was eleven when he became a part of her close-knit family: an obscure twenty-five-year-old New York TV director. Her father, a distinguished film and play writer, had seen one of his low-budget attempts at film directing and immediately sniffed the genius behind the still unpolished product. Always on the lookout for fresh young talent, Robert Montague had agreed to write his next film, and Emma, generous to a fault as usual, offered to star in it: Emma Montague's name was always a sure guarantee of a box-office success.

The film launched Nick Hayward overnight on to the first rank of international film directors.

He had become a regular member of the Montague bustling household and Jo, an only child, immediately adopted him as her special friend. She had even conducted a solemn ceremony in their Hampstead home, in the presence of her parents, baptising Nick her 'god-brother' with ice-cold Perrier mineral water which, she had gathered from commercials, was purer than plain tap water.

Nick stayed often with the Montagues, preferring the noisy, friendly ambiance of their home to the impersonality of London's five-star hotels. When the economic slump brought the British film industry to a halt, he often chose to take his holidays there so as to be near his friends; later he bought a lovely villa in Corfu where the Montagues and many of their close friends spent their summer months.

When Robert Montague died of a heart attack, Nick made it his business to stay in England on every available opportunity, drive down to Brighton where Jo was now attending boarding school, and treat her to lunch or tea and listen to her confessions and problems in place of her dead father. He had become the most important person in her life, beside her mother.

Until just after her sixteenth birthday.

For some time now she had become aware of a marked change in his attitude towards her. It happened quite imperceptibly, so that she could not put her finger as to exactly when he had begun to withdraw. But the signs of the aloofness and odd exasperation were definitely there. And then came that disastrous summer in Corfu which had severed any further contact between them.

She had kept her misery and disillusionment to herself, too ashamed to share it with anyone. But now, after Nick had shown his true character in his beastly treatment of Emma, she had hoped she would at least find an ally in the latter. Yet Emma specifically ordered Jo in her letters to ignore all the ugly rumours and assured her again and again that Nick was and would always be her dearest and most trusted friend.

The dull sound of an object hurled against the wall

shook Jo out of her seething fury. To her amazement, she realised that her hand, as if by its own volition, had flung the innocent brush against the wall in a burst of frustrated rage. It was such an untypical show of temper that she couldn't help giggling. She had always been accused of being too poised, too cool and serene for her age and her chosen vocation in life. Very rarely she allowed the passionate side of her nature to see the light of day. The last time she had done so was three years ago, in Corfu, and the horror of that experience still made her blush with shame. Then too, it had been Nick Hayward who had provoked it.

Jo stood up and shook herself mentally. It was useless and unwise to let that man unsettle her and destroy her single-minded concentration when she was facing one of the most important tests in her life. The only way to combat him, to be revenged, was for her to go through the coming audition, get the part and become an international star. Then she would be powerful enough to face him and fling in his face all her contempt and hatred.

Aware of the time and place, she hurriedly got into her daily uniform of jeans and a freshly laundered shirt, then wasted five precious minutes studying herself in the full-length mirror, trying to see herself in the eyes of her judges: her deep honey-coloured hair, thick and shiny, framed her face which was untouched by make-up, and her large tawny eyes revealed nothing of the anger and anxiety which were still battling inside her. For a moment she regretted having listened to the agent and wished she had put on something less casual. Her long, willowy figure looked its best in her usual uniform of well-cut jeans and a crispy white cotton shirt, but there was something distant and rigid about it that made her look impersonal and untouchable, like a hospital nurse. Her drama school friends always teased her about her taste in clothes: "No man would dare put his arm around you for fear of crushing that beautifully press shirt of yours!"

She read Emma's postcard in the taxi, forgetting its slow painful progress through London's heavy traffic in her concentrated effort to read the real state of Emma's mood between the airy, cheerful lines: 'Having the proverbial wonderful time, but I'm glad you're not here, darling. I'm sure you're doing far better where you are. Impatiently waiting for news. Good luck, my love.'

Jo shivered. It almost seemed as if her mother, even hundreds of miles away, had an uncanny premonition of the incredible events which were taking place in her daughter's life. 'Well, Mum,' she said silently, 'keep your fingers crossed, wherever you are!'

By the time the taxi deposited Jo outside the Staller Agency office building, it was a quarter to eleven and Michael, a young-looking fifty-year-old beanpole of a man, was punishing a meek assistant for Jo's tardy arrival. 'Has no one in that silly academy of yours ever told you that in our business, being late is worse than having a lisp?' he attacked Jo the moment her head appeared at the glass door. 'How dare you keep me and Theodore Ianikis waiting?'

Jo, looking cool and unperturbed in spite of her mad dash up the stairs, caught only the last words. 'Theodore Ianikis?' she breathed. 'Am I going to audition for Ianikis?'

'Of course you are. Didn't I tell you?' Michael was secretly enjoying the impact he had made.

An inaudible gasp escaped Jo's lips: Theodore Ianikis

ran one of the busiest and most successful film and television production companies in the country. It was famous for its many co-productions with foreign companies, mostly from the United States; and while the film industry in England had suffered greatly from the financial recession, almost coming to a halt, Ianikis still managed to churn out at least two films a year.

'Well, aren't you impressed?' the agent prodded impatiently, having expected a greater show of enthusiasm or awe. 'My God, girl, you sure keep a cool head on those slim shoulders of yours! I presume you've heard of Ianikis?'

'Oh, I have,' Jo smiled, having regained her breath. 'And I'm not just impressed—I'm terrified! Does he know I have absolutely no professional experience?'

'Of course he does. But they've all been to see you perform last night and their verdict was favourable, which is quite—'

Jo wouldn't let him finish. 'All? Who else?'

'Oh, the usual crowd: director, scriptwriter, Ianikis himself and me, naturally.' Typically, he got tired of the subject. 'Anyway, we don't have time to chat now. I was hoping I'd have time to coach you a little, but that's out of the question now. You must get there before eleven.' He was pushing Jo unceremoniously out of the office and towards the lifts. 'Fortunately, Ianikis' offices are just across the street. I take it this is your first audition?'

Jo nodded, silently.

'Oh, I suppose you'll do. You can always impress them with that face and body of yours . . . just remember not to lose your cool. They like self-assured, collected beginners.' His shrewd eyes studied the tall girl, taking in the serene beauty and the incredible outward calm which made her so different from the usual type of young hopefuls.

The lift arrived. Jo turned to the older man, her eyes pleading. 'Can't you tell me something about the part? Or at least, the name of the director?'

'You'll find out soon enough. Now in you get, and—' Michael allowed some human emotion to colour his dry, flat bark, 'don't you dare disappoint me . . . or your mother! I'll call you late tonight to tell you the results.'

'Does that mean that you're willing to represent me?' Jo asked, her voice slightly choked. 'I mean, am I on your list now?'

'Of course you are. I've already wasted money and time making a dozen telephone calls on your behalf . . . I'm determined to get my money back. Ten per cent, and no haggling. Is that understood?' And with these ominous words he left Jo to prove herself worthy of such honour.

Ianikis' offices, situated just behind Harrods in a new office building, were designed to impress the successful and to reduce the timid newcomer into awestricken jelly. Ultra-modern Italian furniture, black ebony, chrome and glass rendered the large reception room too austere for a private residence yet too opulent for the usual business premises.

An elderly, well-bred receptionist was obviously expecting her. In a rather archaic upper-class voice, she greeted Jo and showed her into a smaller waiting-room, and suggested she went over the script until the 'gentlemen were ready to see her.'

'Here,' the woman thrust a thick yellow script into Jo's hands, 'you're to read for the girl part—Melissa, I believe the name is. Pages 13 to 17 . . . are you comfortable?'

Jo didn't have to read far to realise that this was every young actress's dream. A gem of a part—Melissa of the title role was a spoilt, naïve yet cunning fifteen-year-old heiress, who was just becoming aware of her feminine prowess and was using it charmingly but dangerously. The plot was set in England, around 1815.

She read the four pages twice over before she became aware of an odd sensation which seemed to grab hold of her, tightening her stomach muscles into a hard, almost painful knot. It was soon interpreted into words: she had to get that part. Melissa seemed to have been written for her and she was ready to pay any price to be allowed to play her. A voice, for years buried away under a blanket of anger and shame, struggled to reach her and finally she could ignore it no longer. It was Nick Hayward's voice, as she remembered it before he had become a stranger, an enemy. Amused, deceptively lazy with its slight American accent: 'Only iron will and ruthless determination stand between a successful star and a failed actress. Talent has little to do with it. And frankly, honey, talented as you are, I don't think you're made of the right stuff. Not tough enough, you see . . . So, if you insist on being an actress, don't expect me to lift a finger to help you. I'd rather see you playing another role in life.'

'I don't need your help, Nick Hayward,' she said silently, unconsciously falling into an old habit of conversing with him internally. 'I'm going to get that part whether you like it or not!'

She was utterly confident now in her own strength, and the conviction helped her relax. She even managed to memorise a few lines, knowing her performance would be far more impressive if she could detach herself from the book. Then, intrigued by the plot and by the character of Melissa, she continued reading past the four pages she was to audition for. It soon dawned on her that Melissa's youthful adventures were told, in short disconnected flashbacks, by Melissa herself at the age of forty-five. Plainly the older Melissa held the larger and far more important part. Jo wondered vaguely who was cast in it.

'I'm sorry, my dear, but I'm afraid the gentlemen are getting a little impatient.' The well-bred voice of the receptionist broke through her thoughts. 'You'll have to go in now.'

A large, sparsely furnished sunny room welcomed her. An enormous glass top table occupied most of the centre space, as if mocking the conventional office desk. Behind it, chewing a huge unlit cigar, Jo recognised the widely-publicised face of Theodore Ianikis, his shiny bald dome and the tinted glasses conforming to his numerous caricatures. Without bothering to remove the cigar from his mouth, the giant smiled and ordered Jo in with a wave of his beringed hand.

'So, you are Josephine Montague,' he remarked.

'Yes,' she said dumbly.

'Rather a long name for such a little thing, isn't it?' the Greek producer chuckled.

'I wouldn't call her little,' said another voice, and Jo turned towards a huge leather settee to face the other presence in the vast, sparse expanses of the office. He was small and fragile just as the producer was large and massive. But what he lacked in stature he filled in with a luxuriant head of thick grey hair. 'She seems very tall to me,' he continued, then turned to address her directly. 'Just to satisfy my curiosity, how tall *are* you?' He seemed deeply intrigued by the question.

'I beg your pardon?' she said in a small voice. She couldn't tell whether they were making fun of her or whether they were just slightly eccentric.

'She's five foot seven, and people call her Jo, for short,' a voice chuckled lightly behind her.

There was no need to turn around. She would have recognised that light voice with its faint American twang even if he were miles away.

Her knees seemed to buckle under her as she swirled around to face him and his arm shot forward to catch her just in time. An electric shock ran through her numb body.

'Hi, honey,' Nicholas Hayward said lightly. 'You look as if you've seen a ghost. Didn't you know you were going to audition for me?'

CHAPTER TWO

HE was so close that she had to raise her head to meet his smiling deep blue gaze, forcing her to respond to the bond of familiarity between them. For a moment she thought she was going to faint. So, probably, did he, for his impersonal touch tightened on her arm and his lazy voice sounded a bit concerned. 'I didn't mean to startle you, honey. Sorry.'

Apart from the occasional photograph in the press or from a safe distant when visiting her mother on film sets, Jo hadn't seen or spoken to him over three years . . . ever since that dreadful night in Corfu. Now, unable to tear her eyes away from that once-loved face, she could discern a few more lines around the eyes and deeper hollows under the strong cheekbones, but otherwise he hadn't changed at all. It was the same deeply tanned and ruggedly chiselled face, the same hard, well-shaped mouth, stretched into that crooked smile. As always, he dismissed the conventional town gear of suit and tie, preferring an open-necked shirt which revealed the strong, straight column of his bronzed neck. She even recognised the tan suede windjacket which hung casually over his broad shoulders. He was at least a head taller than herself, and as always in his proximity, she felt small and slight as if she were still the child he had once used to carry up to bed.

Facing him now, it was hard to believe that this man who loomed so large throughout her growing years, the

23

recipient of so much of her childish love and trust, had treated her so cruelly and only very recently had betrayed her mother. For a moment, she was overwhelmed by an old familiar urge to put out her hand and brush back the glinting pale-gold hair which fell, thick and straight, over his high forehead.

As if reading her thoughts, he raised a hand, pushed his hair back in a well-remembered gesture and then, giving her a friendly pat on the shoulder, turned away from her and strode over to the glass desk, his tall, loose-limbed form leaning lazily against it. With an effort, Jo tore her eyes from that flat, hard chest and the long muscular legs carelessly but disturbingly outlined by the light tan jeans.

'This is Nicholas Hayward,' she heard the Greek producer boom from his place behind the glass table. 'But I don't suppose I need to introduce you. I understand you two are very old friends.'

Released from his suffocating nearness, Jo had found her voice together with the control over her limbs. 'Oh, yes, of course,' she mumbled, trying to convey cool, distant politeness. 'Hello, Mr Hayward.'

'Hi there, *Miss* Montague,' Nicholas Hayward mocked her formal use of his name. 'Don't you ever grow up?'

Jo gaped at him, her eyes darkening in anger and panic. 'What . . . what do you mean?' she asked in a whisper. For a moment she thought he was referring to their very last and stormy encounter.

'Just that you don't seem to have changed at all in three years. You still look sixteen, at the most.'

'Sorry,' she snapped, 'I can't help it.'

'Don't try to,' he retorted, grinning down at her. 'It's just what we need for the film, you see.' And as if that word reminded him what they were all there for, he turned away from her to address his colleagues: 'I've got Peter waiting outside with the camera, so shall we get on with it?' He didn't bother to wait for a reply. 'You've looked at the four pages I marked down for you, haven't you?'

'Judging by the time she took over it, I'd say she'd read the whole damn script twice over,' said the small, grey-headed man who was so interested in her height.

'This is Eric Gardner,' Nicholas said dryly. 'The scriptwriter.'

Jo's face broke into a delighted smile. 'Eric Gardner? My father used to talk a lot about you.'

'Quite right too,' the scriptwriter answered, his eyes smiling at her warmly, belying the dry tone. 'We've been rivals for years and he always managed to grab the better scripts. I miss him a lot.'

'So do I,' Jo said quietly, grateful to find a friend in the room. Though her head was turned away, she sensed Nick's intent gaze fixed on her, demanding contact, but she refused to obey it. It was odd, to be in the same room with the man whom she had once loved almost as much as her father and to be forced, by his own actions, to treat him now as a treacherous stranger.

Eric Gardner was still bent on a brief nostalgic trip. 'Six years since he died, isn't it?' Jo nodded, trying to ignore the pang of dull pain. 'Well, I for one find life much duller without him. No one to compete with. Without him, I'm doomed to a solitary rule as the only great scriptwriter left in the Western hemisphere, and it's so lonely at the top. Isn't that right, Master Hayward?'

Nicholas Hayward ignored the self-mocking boast.

From the corner of her eye, Jo saw him getting busy with a thick yellow script, similar to the one she had been clutching in her hand from the moment she walked in. Ianikis was following her conversation with the scriptwriter with open interest, his eyes twinkling behind their tinted glasses.

'And how is the great Emma?' Eric continued with the same dry, sardonic tone which didn't hide a deep admiration. 'I haven't seen her in months!'

The silence which followed his casual remark couldn't be ignored, even by him.

'What's the matter?' he asked, irritably. 'Have I said something wrong?'

Jo turned to look at Nick Hayward, her eyes hard and brilliant. 'Why don't you ask Mr Hayward that? I haven't seen my mother for weeks, but I understand that he keeps in constant touch with her.'

'She's fine,' Nick Hayward answered calmly, answering her hard look with an impersonal, opaque one. 'Enjoying a sorely needed rest. And incidentally, Jo, she sends you her love. You should write her more often, you know.'

'I would,' she retorted, her voice barely above a whisper, 'if the postbox she's given me was less objectionable.'

'What in the name of heaven are you two talking about?' the bewildered scriptwriter exploded.

Jo no longer cared about getting the part of Melissa. Working under the hateful directorship of Nick Hayward was too high a price to pay, she decided. 'Oh, don't you know?' she turned to Eric Gardner. 'My mother was supposed to star in Mr Hayward's latest film but apparently she didn't satisfy his high artistic requirements . . . too tired, I understand was the official reason, wasn't it, Mr Hayward?' Her voice rang falsely bright and polite in the still room.

She was still smarting with the memory of the day, four weeks ago, when one of her classmates brought her the evening paper, noted for its vulgar eagerness for showbiz scandals:

'So Nicholas Hayward doesn't want your mother in his film! I thought Emma Montague was too big a star to fall victim to a director's whim.'

'What are you talking about?' Jo asked.

'This . . .' The girl thrust the paper into Jo's hand. 'This is what I'm talking about, and don't tell me you know nothing about it!'

It was a short, vitriolic item: 'Emma Montague, one of our most cherished actresses, has been given the boot by director Nicholas Hayward after eight years of successful and lucrative collaboration. Miss Montague will not star in his new, as yet unnamed film. When asked about his motives, the thirty-four-year old genius remained his usual aloof self but refrained from denying the rumour. We understand from very reliable sources that Miss Montague's role might be offered to the beautiful Andrea Burton who has been seen recently in the company of the acclaimed director. Shooting of the film has been postponed for the time being, says the great Hayward. Miss Emma Montague herself was unavailable for comment.'

The more respectable press didn't endorse the sensational news item. The official word was that Emma Montague had taken a long vacation after a strenuous year of filming and stage work and that Nicholas Hayward had agreed to release her from her contract. But

Jo, knowing and hating Nick Hayward as she did, had opted to take the gossip columnist's version.

Angry tears of frustration were threatening to break her coolly composed face as it occurred to her that she would now have to relinquish her first great chance because the man who offered it was none other than her sworn enemy.

Aware of the unnatural silence in the large office, she turned to Nicholas Hayward, her furious eyes belying her cool, polite voice. 'I'm surprised to see that you're now bent on a new project, Mr Hayward. I've gathered from the press that you were determined to carry on with the other film, though with another star . . . Andrea Burton, I believe was the name mentioned.'

'Is that what you've gathered?' Hayward retorted, mimicking her falsely polite interest, 'Well, *Miss* Montague, I suggest you learn to ignore the press if you wish to pursue a career as an actress.'

'Thank you, sir,' she said, 'I'll try and remember that.'

Theodore Ianikis had had enough of the game. 'I hate interrupting you two,' he cut in briskly, showing a glimpse of the hardened producer behind the beaming, goodnatured equanimity, 'but I would like to get down to business. This is supposed to be an audition, not a reunion.'

Nicholas Hayward nodded curtly and turned to his producer: 'Sure, if Miss Montague is ready. But it seems to me she would rather not be working with me at all . . . not after the way I've been treating her mother, as she "has gathered from the press".' He was speaking to the others, but his dangerously sparkling gaze was fixed coldly on her.

Jo was tempted to agree. Yet, as she stared at the

three men, all watching her blankly, she suddenly knew that this would be madness. Personal feelings were an extravagant luxury in show business. Only the part, only success counted . . . and to hell with what one felt about the rest. Both her mother and Nicholas Hayward had been drumming this rule into her head for years.

'I'm sorry if that's the impression I gave,' she reverted to her usual collected manner. 'I'd. like very much to read for you, Mr Hayward, that is if you—'

He reacted with a short, humourless laugh. 'That's the spirit, honey! Don't let any moral scruples stand in the way of your ambition!'

She went pale. Nothing he could say would have been more painful or, to her shame, more accurate. 'Oh, let's get on with it,' he broke the silence irritably. 'You'll read for us once and then we'll give you a short screen test. I'm flying back to the States tomorrow, so I'm afraid we'll have to squeeze everything into one morning.'

The hard angry glint in his eyes had been replaced by the professional impatience to get on with the business at hand. Suddenly he was transformed into a stranger, a man she had never seen before: authoritative, intimidating yet at the same time transmitting something of his nervous energy into her numb body. She was too fascinated by the change in him to fully digest the fact that she was about to face another ordeal, far worse than a mere reading audition: a screen test.

'What do you want me to do?' She forced her voice to sound professional and detached, though she felt her stomach muscles tighten as he came to stand by her.

'Let see now . . . you'd better sit down somewhere. You don't look very relaxed standing up like this.' He managed to convey an exasperated criticism. 'Go and sit

beside Eric.' Jo obeyed the slight push of his hand and
went to her place, sinking into the huge settee. 'You'll
feed her the lines, Eric, won't you?'

The writer mumbled his reluctant agreement. 'Shall
we start, then?' he asked.

'Let me brief her first,' said Nicholas, turning to Jo.
'Melissa is very young, very rich and spoilt rotten, yet at
the same time she's disarmingly charming. The scene
you're about to read is between her and her guardian, Sir
John, who is secretly in love with her and is deeply
ashamed of what he considers a perverted passion for a
girl he has been bringing up since infancy.' Nicholas
Hayward stopped for a second and looked at her intently. 'Melissa, as you probably gathered already, is very
well aware of it and quite ruthlessly toys with his weak-
ness. She'll finally return his love, but only after her life
has been almost ruined by the seduction of an equally
ruthless cavalry officer.' He paused for a second. 'You
noticed, I suppose, that all this is told in flashbacks by
Melissa herself at the age of forty-five. You won't be
playing that part, naturally.'

Jo had already gathered that, but her heart leaped to
her throat as she noticed that he hadn't used the con-
ditional form. He was speaking as if the part was already
hers.

'Think you could do it, Jo?'

It took a second before she realised the question was
addressed to her. She gulped. 'I . . . I'd like to try,' she
said firmly.

'Well, why not?' Nick suggested. 'Start at . . . let's see
now . . . yes, top of page 13. All right?' Jo nodded,
crisply. 'Right, then. Take your time. Ready when you
are.'

Swallowing hard, she opened the script and hardly pausing for a fresh breath, delivered her first line, turning to look at Eric, beside her.

'"It's dreadful,"' she stammered. '"It's really quite dreadful, and yet I've never felt so happy before, John."'

'Hold it!'

Nicholas Hayward's voice cut in, sharp and cold as ice. Jo looked up at him, confused.

'You're supposed to be a well-bred nineteenth-century girl, just out of the schoolroom, Jo, not a spoilt modern Hampstead brat. This is a period film, not a suburban melodrama.' His eyes bored into hers, as if trying to drum his criticism into her brain. 'I saw you last night as Joan of Arc, a medieval peasant girl. Well, try and put yourself now in the shoes of Melissa . . . Think of Jane Austen's Emma.' He was knowingly, cruelly mentioning the name of her favourite heroine which also happened to be that of her mother's. 'Does that ring a familiar bell?'

'Yes,' she whispered, hating him and at the same time pleading with him silently to be less harsh with her, show her something of his old fatherly patience.

'Start again,' he ordered dryly. 'But perhaps . . .' Suddenly he was alive again. 'That's it! Why don't you slip down on the floor? Yes, like that . . . Now, lean against Eric's knees and don't try to look up at him when you talk. Look at me.' Jo obeyed him. 'All right, now try again. And this time put some real feelings into it. Okay?'

Jo ordered herself to relax. Kneeling as she was with her back against the settee, she could not turn away from the three coldly staring men. So instead she shut her eyes and systematically forced her heart and rushing blood to calm down. Finally, when she was relieved of the debilitating stage fright, she opened her eyes, looked at her director and started again.

'That'll do!'

It took Jo several seconds to emerge from 1815 England and resurface in Ianikis' lavish office, occupied by three unsmiling men. Her eyes focused on the tall, lazily relaxed form of the man who had interrupted her and was shaken by a sudden wave of deep embarrassment: in the scene she had just read, she had been talking about her awakening love for a young earl and her determination to show him that she was no longer a child but a full-grown woman. She was sure now that Nicholas Hayward had made her face him and say her lines directly at him so as to render the makebelieve situation almost real: it was almost as if Jo, not Melissa, was confessing her long-forgotten love for Nick, who was hiding somewhere behind the granite rock of the world-famous film director, Nicholas Hayward.

Both Ianikis and Eric Gardner were watching him intently. He himself seemed lost in speculation. Jo was ignored. No one bothered to tell her whether she had done well or not. She remained kneeling where she was, uncomfortably aware of the cramp in her knees, yet not daring to move or change her position.

'Well?' Theodore Ianikis finally ventured to break the silence. 'What's the verdict, maestro?'

Hayward ignored him. 'Are you free for the rest of the day?' he asked Jo dryly.

Jo stiffened. She had forgotten all about the time. She was due for another performance of *Saint Joan*. 'Not really,' she apologised. 'I have a matinée at three.'

Nicholas glanced at his wrist watch. 'You'd better be going, then. Do you have an agent?' he asked, dryly.

She swallowed. 'Yes, it's—it's Michael Staller.'

'Oh, yes. Well, we'll get in touch with him once I've made my decision.' He was polite, impersonal and impatient to get rid of her.

She was near tears. Obviously he had decided against taking her. He had forgotten all about the screen test he had mentioned before.

She rose stiffly to her feet. The faces of both the producer and the scriptwriter were blank, as if they had pulled a mask over them. 'May I go, then?' she managed to murmur.

'Oh, yes, yes,' Nicholas dismissed her. 'Thank you,' he added as an afterthought.

Her attention was on the three men, so she didn't notice the fourth who was standing by the door, and as luck would have it, she had to ruin an already shaky exit by colliding into him.

'Sorry,' she gasped, and stepped back.

He was quite young, perhaps in his mid-twenties, with short curly red hair and an attractively ugly freckled face; his open smile was a great comfort after the deadpan looks on her judges. 'You'd better be careful, darling,' he chuckled at her. 'This camera holds very precious material. You don't want to go through the whole ordeal again, do you, now?'

Only now she spotted the hand-held TV camera he was cradling against his chest as if it were a precious child. As realisation slowly dawned on her, she turned around and stared questioningly at Nick Hayward.

'Oh, didn't you notice?' he answered her unspoken enquiry. 'Peter was taping the whole audition. I thought you'd be more comfortable if we didn't drag you to the studio for an additional screen test.' He gave her an almost human smile. 'We'll watch your test now on the video recorder here and then let your agent know what we think.' He turned to converse with the cameraman before she was out of the room.

Alone once again in the small room where she had been preparing for her audition, Jo sank into the deep armchair and waited for her heart to resume a more normal pace.

She still wanted desperately to play the part of Melissa, but her desire was overshadowed by a far more disturbing emotion: the almost suffocating wish to be allowed to work with Nicholas Hayward. It no longer mattered that he had been so beastly towards her mother . . . she even forgot how he had humiliated and shamed her three years ago. There was no connection between the man she had once known and the stranger for whom she had just been performing her heart out. All she wanted was to be given the chance to spend a few months under the inspiring and exciting guidance of this ingenious director.

The sound of Eric Gardner's belligerent voice rose shrilly from behind the door she had neglected to shut properly. 'Good God, Hayward! She doesn't only look like Emma—she can even act like her. I know you hate the idea, Nick, but this girl is definitely your Melissa.'

She couldn't hear Nick's response, which was given in a low voice, but Ianikis' voice boomed instead:

'What have you got against the girl, my friend? She's perfect, and her resemblance to Emma Montague is absolutely astounding. She also seems very cool and level-headed to me. So I do not think you'll have any trouble with her, even if she's still only a drama-school greenhorn.'

Jo listened, frozen in her seat. A small voice inside her was pleading silently with Nick Hayward to give in and cast her as Melissa. She had no idea why he was vehemently against using her: it could have been his guilt concerning her mother, but she knew him better than that. Nick had no scruples when it came to his art. She could only deduce that he was either displeased with her performance, or worse . . . he still held her in contempt because of that night on the Corfu beach.

She gasped as the door broke open and Nick Hayward stormed out, his face white with repressed fury. 'What are you doing here?' he demanded tightly when he spotted her. 'Were you eavesdropping?'

'I . . . I just needed a moment to collect myself,' she stammered her apologies. 'Oh, all right,' he muttered. 'But it's no use your waiting here. You better go back to your academy, or you'll miss your matinée.'

Without a smile or a word of comfort, he turned his back on her and was about to leave the room.

Jo couldn't help herself. 'Is it . . . is it because of the way I behaved that night?' Anger made her voice almost ugly.

He turned back, his face hard, ignoring any prior relationship. 'What the hell are you on about, Jo?'

'I heard you in there. You don't want me in your film . . . They thought I was good, but you still don't want me. Why? Is it because of me, or because of what you've done to my mother?'

For a moment he gaped at her, then with an impatient shrug he snapped: 'Hell, Jo. You should know by now that I never allow personal feelings to interfere with my decisions. If you're good for my film, you'll get the part. If not—' He stopped and gave her an opaque look which filled her with misery. 'Oh, why don't you grow up?'

Back at the Academy Jo said nothing about the audition. Somehow she managed to go through the afternoon matinée and the evening performance, and the fact that she had managed to give almost as good a performance as the night before said a lot for her professional singlemindedness. But the moment she came off stage, she was nervous, irritable and restless, surprising both herself and her schoolmates. She was famous, often disliked, for her unshaken composure and lack of temperament. Well, at last she showed she was truly a member of the acting community. The general opinion was that her success had gone to her head. She left it at that.

Oddly enough, instead of tormenting herself with the question of whether or not she had got the part, she spent the time chewing over Nick Hayward's violent reluctance to cast her. She almost forgot that only a few hours ago she herself had sworn that she would never agree to work with him. She was also uncomfortably puzzled by the producer's and the scriptwriter's cryptic remarks concerning her uncanny resemblance to Emma. By the time she returned to the empty Hampstead house, she was exhausted, and depressed and totally out of her depth. 'I don't care if I don't get Melissa,' she told herself, and almost meant it. No part was worth such torture of uncertainty.

Michael Staller phoned her after midnight to tell her, in a most matter-of-fact manner, that the part was hers.

'Come down to Ianikis' office tomorrow to sign your contract. I think I got you the best possible terms, considering the fact that this is your first professional venture. You'll be filming on location . . . somewhere in the Chilterns, half an hour from Stratford . . . and you're starting in four weeks' time, so you'd better tell the Academy that you won't be finishing the year with them. Come and see me tomorrow, after you sign the contract. Goodnight and good luck . . .' Jo felt a swell of warm gratitude as she heard the unusual warmth in this dry, unemotional man's voice. 'I'm counting on you, Jo, and so is your mother, so do it well.'

The large Hampstead house felt very barren and gloomy. Madge had moved out a few months ago into a nearby flat and for the first time Jo wished she had asked a school friend to come and stay with her so as to dispel the vast emptiness.

She had never missed Emma as badly as she had that night. She needed to talk to her, tell her about her doubts, about the confusing mixture of elation and self-disgust. She knew Emma would have been delighted with her for landing such a wonderful part as Melissa, yet she needed to hear her say so . . . to reassure her that she didn't think badly of her for agreeing to work with the man who had caused her such pain and unhappiness. But Emma was away, probably licking her wounds in some remote tropical paradise, and she, Jo, had to cope all alone with her tormented conscience and her contradicting feelings for Nick.

Like Emma, sleep too was a hundred miles away, and Jo kept wandering about the house, trying to find some corner where she would feel at peace. Finally she settled with a mug of tea in her father's study. It was a small cosy room, open only to closest friends. Nick Hayward had once been amongst those.

Forget Nick, she ordered herself. Remember only Nicholas Hayward who is going to launch you on a brilliant acting career.

But how could she? Even sitting in the old armchair by the dead fireplace, she could see his long relaxed form, stretched along the settee, and could hear his lazy drawl discussing with her his next film, his latest girl-friend, jokingly berating a producer who was proving to be something of a moron.

Smiling ruefully, Jo looked down on the large, masculine T-shirt which disguised the feminine curves of her upper body, exposing only the smooth length of her legs. It had reached down to her ankles when Nick had given it to her—a plain, awkward child of eleven.

He had been staying in the house, in his old room, separated from her nursey by a bathroom which they shared. She woke up in the middle of the night, dreadfully thirsty and too sleepy to go down to the kitchen. So she groped her way to the bathroom for a drink of water and had been so startled to find him in the tub that she tripped and fell into the warm water, with him. They had both thought it was madly amusing and they laughed about it for years. It was then that Nick had given her one of his T-shirts to replace the soaking nightgown, and Jo had never used conventional nightwear since.

'Stop it,' she scolded herself, almost spilling the tea in her irritation. 'Stop thinking about him, for heaven's sake!'

But the memory was back, refusing to be swept back under the carpet now that she had met Nick again and

was facing weeks of seeing him daily. It was the last
memory she had of him . . . a memory she had been
struggling to repress for three long years . . .

They had been spending the summer at Nick's villa in
Corfu, as they did every year. It was a glorious month of
sun and sea and late nights, with both Emma and Nick
unhindered by any film commitments. The house was
full of old friends and Nick was enjoying one of his
lighthearted, shortlived affairs with a stunning Swiss
actress. Jo felt particularly happy that summer since
Nick, who had been avoiding her for many months now,
treated her quite kindly, almost as if he had overcome
his odd objection to her. Besides, she was about to
start her last year at school and was already looking
forward to her forthcoming drama training and her
career.

Jo and Emma were going back to London the next
day, and to celebrate their last night Nick's housekeeper
had prepared a sumptuous Greek meal which left all the
guests in a happy stupor, content just to sit around and
enjoy each other's company. And suddenly Jo felt like a
last midnight swim in the calm, warm Mediterranean
water. No one seemed keen on the idea; the only other
midnight-swim fan was Nick, who had disappeared
soon after dinner with his Swiss girl-friend, Nadia. So Jo
went out alone, wearing a tiny crocheted bikini which
she had been given that very day by Nadia as a con-
descending gift. It was Jo's first bikini and she was loath
to leave the island without trying it at least once, even if
at night and without any audience.

It was a dark night and the water was wonderfully soft
and warm. She swam for a good twenty minutes before
she turned back to the beach. She was still wading in the

water, her feet hardly touching sand, when she saw two dark silhouettes on the sand, near enough for her to recognise them. It was Nick and Nadia.

To her embarrassment, she realised that they were kissing, Nadia crouching beside Nick who was lying on his back. They were certainly not in the mood for company. In the still summer night, their voices carried easily over the short distance.

'Let's go in, Nicky,' Nadia suggested, the invitation quite unmistaken in her low, husky voice.

'Not right now, honey,' Nick answered lazily. 'I'm too comfortable here.'

'Well,' the actress's voice sounded slightly petulant, 'I'm getting chilly. I'm going in to get a sweater.'

'Why don't you stay indoors?' He didn't seem very eager for her company right now. 'I'll see you later in your room.'

The water was getting uncomfortably cold and Jo waited impatiently for Nadia to reach the villa so she could come out. It would have been far too awkward for them all if she had interrupted the scene while Nadia was still there.

Nick remained lying on the sand, and for a moment she thought of joining him for a nice, friendly chat. But suddenly she felt ridiculously mischievous and light-headed, if only because he didn't seem to be terribly in love with the sultry Nadia.

She swam a few yards along the beach, and came out quite a distance away from him. By circumventing his prostrate body, she managed to approach him un-noticed, from behind. It had taken her a good ten minutes to reach him. Once there, she knelt down and kissed him lightly on the forehead.

'Nadia?' he mumbled lazily, not bothering to open his eyes.

'Aha,' Jo chuckled throatily, giving an excellent imitation of Nadia's kittenish gurgle. She and Nick had often indulged in makebelieve scenes, where they would improvise particularly melodramatic or camp situations and Jo proved to be extremely adept at imitating overemotional actresses. 'You're wet!' Nick sounded vaguely surprised as his arm came back over his head and inadvertently touched her wet crocheted bikini. 'I thought you said you were going up to bed . . . not change into a bikini and take a swim.'

'I changed my mind, *chéri*,' Jo breathed in his ear, a gurgle of laughter already beginning to surface and spoil her perfect personification of Nadia.

'Mmm . . . delicious,' he murmured, his voice caressing her, like the soft warm breeze: 'I can't resist wet skin . . . come here.'

She was utterly unprepared for his next move. The hand which was wandering lightly over her wet midriff suddenly tightened around her waist, pulling her from behind, so that she was now half kneeling, half bending over him, while his other hand pulled her head down until it was level with his own. She stifled a giggle as she felt her lips being pressed against his, not crushingly, but certainly not in the butterfly kisses he used to give her when she was a child.

Still enjoying her successful deception, she was about to free her mouth long enough to tell him that he had been had, that instead of Nadia he was actually kissing her, Jo, when suddenly a wave of warm liquid seemed to erupt somewhere inside her and gush forcibly through her veins. Tentatively, no longer giggling, she savoured the touch of Nick's exploring mouth, revelling as she did so in the new, never before experienced sensuality of her reaction. It was a wonderful first kiss, sweet, endless, demanding her total participation, making her forget where she was and ignore the implications of it. She was only aware of Nick's hard, warm hands holding her head tightly and his lips taking possession of her, devouring her whole being.

'Jo?' she heard him gasp her name huskily. 'Oh, my God . . . it's you!'

She didn't want to talk. All she wanted was to drown once more in the blissful sweetness of his kiss. Hardly aware of what she was doing, she let her body slide next to his, stretching to its full length so that she could feel his naked, flat chest and smooth, long muscular legs, against her bare, still wet body, and ignoring the deep, tortured groan which escaped his lips, she found his mouth again and forgot everything in the engulfing whirlpool of another deep, exploring, exhilarating kiss.

A faint warning bell was ringing in a far corner of her intoxicated consciousness, as she arched to fit her body against his, cradling into it in an attempt to be swallowed within it; his body seemed to be changing, subtly . . . growing more taut and hungry every second. And that odd transformation kindled her already inflamed sensuality into a blazing fire, exhilarating yet at the same time frightening.

'Nicky,' she gasped when he finally tore his mouth away from hers. 'That . . . that was—ah!'

A gasp broke her exclamation in mid-word. He had pushed her away from him in one cruel, painful stroke, almost knocking the air out of her lungs.

'You . . . you little bitch!'

The ugly word, never used against her by anyone, let alone by Nick, was even more painful than the push. She remained lying on the sand, her eyes large and frightened as she saw him sit up and kneel above her. 'What the hell did you think you were doing?'

'It was . . . it was in fun,' she stammered, reeling between the still heady tingling of his kiss and his new, terrifying fury.

'In fun?' His face was shrouded by the dark night, but the voice was icy with cold contemptuous anger. 'Were you experimenting on me, Jo?'

'No, no . . . I was just pretending to be Nadia, and you—'

Nick wouldn't let her finish; 'Well then, how far are you ready to carry this experiment, Jo?'

'Please, Nicky,' she was almost sobbing now, 'I didn't mean to . . . to kiss you. Only pretend—' Involuntarily, she reached a hand to touch him, try and reassure him that she was still the Jo he had always liked.

'Oh, no!' He slapped her hand away. 'Not with me, you don't. That's what the boys of your own age are there for . . . to experiment with. I'm too busy and definitely not old or depraved enough to find myself facing a judge and accused of interfering with an underage Lolita like you.'

'I'm . . . I'm not under-aged,' she stammered, foolishly hanging on to one utterly irrelevant detail. 'I'm sixteen and three months—'

He groaned audibly. Furious contempt had distorted the good humoured, handsome features; the deep blue eyes were hard and cold and sparkling dangerously. Jo shut her eyes with a shudder as a sense of nauseating shame engulfed her.

'Go home, Jo,' he hissed at her. 'I owe your mother too much to do to you what I feel like doing right now . . .' Seeing her eyes widen, he laughed humourlessly. 'Oh, no . . . not what you're thinking, honey . . . I meant giving you the thrashing of your life!'

She could only stare at him, aware of a new emotion budding deep within her: something hard and ugly. 'I hate you,' she heard herself say, her mind interpreting that utterly new feeling into words. 'I hate you, Nicky!'

'Good for you. As long as you keep it that way, we're both better off.' He was on his feet now, and towering over her, his face no longer discernible in the dark.'

'I'm going back,' he announced. 'You'd better wait here a few moments, then go to the house and put something on. All I need now is for Emma to accuse me of keeping you out at night and making you catch cold.' He stared her in silence for a moment. 'But I warn you, Jo . . . don't you ever do that again. Not with me I don't believe in half-measures. Next time you come experimenting with me or with any other guy my age, you'd better be prepared to go the whole way . . . under-aged virgin or not!'

'Shut up!'

Back in the small study in Hampstead, Jo buried her head in the cushions and vented all her penned-up anger, humiliation and pain in that cry. To her own amazement, she realised that she was sobbing, bitterly, loudly. She had become so cool, so detached and cautious after that night with him; a far cry from the lively excitable girl she had been until then. She now knew why: he had hurt her as no one had ever done before, and she was determined that no one, no man, would ever hurt her again like that.

CHAPTER THREE

FROM its hilly, isolated perch, Elmfield Manor ruled supreme over a magnificent vista of luscious green lawns, landscaped gardens, even a small lake, protected by a girdle of thick woods. The Manor itself, built by an admirer of John Nash, was a very lovely sample of Georgian architecture, its pure classical lines and gleaming white façade proudly compensating for its modest dimensions.

It was twilight when Jo parked her tired old Mini in the gravelled front courtyard, glancing ruefully at the two outrageously extravagant foreign sports cars which were already parked there. A huge, closed van which she had passed some two miles away was pulling in after her, its rough loud engine breaking the peaceful timelessness of the setting and forcing the twentieth century into this relic of bygone grace.

Her heart pounding excitedly at the prospect of spending the next few weeks in such delightful surroundings, Jo stepped out of the car and started walking towards the large gleaming oak doors of the main entrance, leaving her suitcase behind. On her drive up the hills, she had noticed a small village with one inn and she guessed the film crew and the cast would be installed there for the duration of the film.

She reached the wide stone steps, the massive oak door burst open and a child, its minute body swallowed in baggy khaki trousers and a huge sweat shirt, came rushing out to meet Jo halfway.

'Hi,' the child said in a strong American accent. The voice and the large smiling eyes betrayed its sex. It was a girl; a young woman rather, but her resemblance to a modern version of Puck was quite uncanny. 'I'm Lindsey, the production assistant.'

'Don't try to glamorise yourself, lovey,' said a man who came out after her. 'You're old Nick's dogsbody, and that's good enough for you.'

'Hello,' Jo smiled at the girl. 'I'm Jo Monta—'

'We know who you are,' said the man, giving her a wide smile which lit his freckled face in a vaguely familiar way. 'My name is Peter . . . and I believe we have met already, in Ianikis' office, when you came for your audition—'

'Of course,' she suddenly remembered. 'You were the one with the camera . . . I'm terribly sorry, but—'

'Don't be silly.' Lindsey waved her apology aside. 'You were in no state to notice anyone in that room, and besides, nobody recognises Peter without his precious camera. Where's your luggage?' she continued, hardly pausing for breath.

'In the car,' Jo answered 'I thought you'd want me to take it to the hotel or . . .'

'This *is* the hotel.' Lindsey looked at her a little bemused.

'Elmfield Manor?' Jo stared amazed at the lovely entrance hall. 'I thought we were going to use it as the film location . . . Melissa's home.'

'That's right . . . but you're also going to stay here throughout the shooting.'

'A hotel?' Jo repeated, amazed. 'We'll be shooting the film in a hotel?'

'What's wrong with that? It used to be the private residence of an ancient aristocratic family. Now the two sons are running it as a very exclusive hotel for the discerning rich . . . you'll love it, I promise you.'

'Oh, I'm sure, but—'

'Here, let me have the keys to the boot,' Peter interrupted, 'and I'll get your luggage for you.'

'Oh, I can carry it myself,' Jo objected.

'Let him, sweetie,' Lindsey advised her. 'This is your last chance of being treated as a lady . . . or as a human being, for that matter. From tomorrow you'll be nothing but a puppet, a dummy, a house pet—'

'A film actress,' Peter summed it all in one word. 'So let me have the keys, lovey.' Jo stopped arguing.

'Come on, Jo,' Lindsey was propelling her cheerfully into the large scantily but tastefully furnished main hall.' Let me show you to your room and brief you on house rules. From then on, you're on your own, I'm afraid.'

The place was swarming with people carrying every conceivable variety of lighting and film equipment and looking as if the fate of the universe depended on their swift action. As she passed the reception desk, which was actually a large Chippendale dining-table, Theodore Ianikis was conducting an earnest conversation with the hotel manager. Lindsey wouldn't allow her to stop and say hello.

'You'll meet them all afterwards, Jo. Everybody is too busy right now to notice you. It's always a madhouse on the night before the first day of shooting.' Unceremoniously, she kept pushing Jo up the graceful curving staircase.

'It's a beautiful house,' Jo congratulated Lindsey as she followed her along the first floor corridor. 'That's exactly what I imagined Melissa's home to be like. But wouldn't the hotel guests be annoyed by a large film crew running around the place?'

'There *are* no other guests, sweetie,' Lindsey assured her. 'Nick made Ianikis rent the place, bedrooms, reception rooms and grounds for the sole purpose of his artistic needs. The place will be closed for the duration of the shooting, though some of the staff will still be around to take care of Nick Hayward's worldly comforts . . .'

'Or yours,' Jo reminded her mildly. In spite of her own sizzling resentment, she still bristled whenever anyone spoke disparagingly of Nicholas Hayward.

'Oh, no, love, not me. Only you—that is, Nick and the stars. We underlings are housed in and about the estate . . . the staff accommodation. Very nice and comfortable, even if they are only for the servants. Very different from the desert tent I had in my last film. There you are—'

She opened the door at the end of the corridor and pushed Jo in. 'There are only ten rooms with bathrooms in this dump. I'm afraid you'll have to share the bathroom with Andrea Burton.'

Jo was admiring the sky-blue décor of the Regency-style bedroom, with its large poster-bed and the graceful tall Georgian windows. But her attention was caught sharply by the name. Andrea Burton was the star who, according to that gossip item, was Emma Montague's natural replacement as Hayward's leading lady. Jo remembered, seething, the casual allusion to the romantic attachment of the director and the young star. 'Andrea Burton?' She turned on Lindsey, trying to hide her indignation. 'I didn't know she was in this too.'

'Oh, but she is . . . and she won't let you forget it either,' Lindsey giggled.

Jo frowned. 'But I don't remember any other large female part . . . I mean, Andrea Burton couldn't possibly agree to—' She stopped. 'Unless she's playing the part of the older Melissa.'

'You must be joking!' Lindsey laughed shortly. 'Andrea Burton playing the part of a forty-five-year-old matron? You wouldn't catch her dead in anything a day older than thirty! No, sweetie, she's playing the part of Helena, Sir John's—your guardian's—wife.'

'But that's a tiny part.' Jo looked puzzled. 'Hardly any meat on it at all—' She remembered vaguely a scene where Helena, the estranged wife, returns home and has a resounding argument with Sir John.

'Not any more, it isn't. It's a nice juicy part now. A genuine show-stopper.'

Jo's elated mood had gone sour. Nick Hayward had obviously offered the actress this part as a compensation prize. After all, she had lost the star role in his discarded film. Andrea Burton was a British actress who had moved to Hollywood, but like many other stars, she plainly wasn't averse to a cameo part which demanded only a few days of shooting but which put her name at the top of the bill and offered her a very substantial sum of money. Beside, Jo remarked acidly to herself, Nick Hayward had probably made sure his recent girl-friend had a legitimate reason for being on set with him.

'And she's staying in the next room to mine?' she asked, not hiding her displeasure.

'That's right, but she won't bother you much. She hardly has four shooting days . . . though I bet she'll try and wheedle a few more scenes out of Nick.' The other girl's grin didn't give Andrea much hope of achieving this. 'Anyway, she isn't here yet, and I'm afraid there's going to be some trouble when she hears she has to share a bathroom with you; but this is my problem, not yours,' Lindsey ended hurriedly. 'I'm sorry, sweetie, but I really can't stay and chat. I'm rushed off my feet today, with everyone arriving and nobody knowing what's where and why . . .' She was already outside the room.

'Lindsey,' Jo stopped her, 'who *is* going to play the older Melissa?'

The girl paused uneasily before she answered: 'We don't know. Nick is still considering several possibilities.'

'Isn't it a bit odd? After all, the older Melissa is the star part. I mean, how could Nick start shooting without—'

'Let me give you a bit of advice, sweetie,' Lindsey interrupted her shortly. 'Don't attempt to make sense out of anything Nick does or doesn't do. He's a law unto himself—which is hardly surprising. He is, after all, a genius.'

Jo didn't stay in her room. It was still early and she was eager to meet her fellow actors and get to know her home for the next few weeks.

People were still rushing in and out of the main hall, cursing softly as she kept getting in their way. Feeling definitely de trop, she finally escaped into a small deserted lounge, with a huge blazing Adam fireplace as its focus. A folding formica-top table, utterly out of place in the elegant nineteenth-century surroundings, looked highly tempting with the large coffee pot and appetising sandwiches, which reminded her how hungry she was.

'Hello there,' a beautifully modulated and deep voice floated towards her from the depth of a high-backed armchair. 'And who might you be?'

'Jo . . .' she stammered, startled. 'Jo Montague.'

'As if I didn't know,' the voice said, and now she could see the face which went with it. She recognised it immediately, having seen it often enough on the TV screen. Bracing herself, she waited for him to ask about her relation to Emma Montague. The prospect of having people talking to her about her mother, perhaps even offering their condolences for the way she'd been treated, was rather disturbing. But to her relief, her new colleague said nothing.

'Would you like some of this?' he asked instead, raising his arm to show her a large tumbler half filled with amber-coloured drink. 'Mediocre whisky, but quite drinkable.' He was about thirty-five, handsome in a donnish sort of way, with intelligent, sensitive features. His voice, though, was his greatest asset, even drunk as he seemed to be at the moment.

'No, thank you,' Jo assured him, feeling quite at ease with him. He reminded her of the actors she met at her parents' home: seasoned and successful if slightly theatrical. 'I'd rather have coffee and something to eat.'

'Have a sandwich, then.' He rose to his feet and walked over to the table, offering her the sandwich plate. 'I'm afraid dinner is still something in the near but vague future. First day's hassle, they assure me. I'm Francis Blakely, incidentally—Sir John in your script.'

'How do you do?' Jo smiled, and solemnly shook hands with him. She felt comfortably at ease with this friendly if somewhat tipsy actor.

'I do very well, considering the fact that I'm starving

and not too impressed by the choice of drinks in this place. Here, let me pour you a cup of coffee.'

'Pour one for me too, mate,' another voice broke in from behind them, and they both turned around.

Two black eyes were boring into hers from one of the most handsome faces she had ever seen. The man looked like a painting of Lord Byron, sporting the same curly, windblown hair-style and an open-necked, wide-collared shirt which showed off his smooth, pale chest. 'Hello, lover . . .' he whispered as his arm slipped around her waist, 'meet your seducer.'

'Hello, seducer.' Jo fell easily into the artificial banter of her species which she had learnt at drama school.

He didn't bother to introduce himself. Darren Williams was too well known a star to trouble with such social trivialities.' I was hoping to meet you in London, get acquainted, like, if you get my meaning . . .' His arm tightened, bringing her body closer to his. 'But I'm afraid I was kept busy filming in Corsica until yesterday. Dreadful movie, too.'

'That's all right,' Jo said lightly. 'I'm sure we'll have plenty of time to get acquainted here.'

'Only if we spend lots of time together, starting from right now. We don't want Nicholas God Hayward getting impatient with us on set, do we? We'd better come all prepared—lines, moves and . . . familiarity?'

Jo blushed. Her scenes with him were already a source of endless embarrassment to her. Going over the script with the writer, Eric Gardner, she had become aware of the intimate situations she was in for, in the role of Melissa. The most explicitly sensual were with Darren Williams, who was playing the dashing officer—her seducer.

'Call-sheets, folks.' Lindsey came hurrying in, waving a bunch of papers, still wearing those baggy khaki trousers and the huge sweat shirt. 'You're all on. Make-up at six, I'm afraid. You're first, Jo—sorry.'

'Six o'clock? On the first day?' Darren exploded.

'Sorry,' Lindsey twinkled. 'You know what it's like shooting a film in England. You have to grab every hour of sunshine . . .'

'Oh, spare me the details,' Darren mumbled, and withdrew to one of the deep armchairs.

Lindsey remained unruffled by his bad-tempered display. 'They're serving dinner now in the kitchen. I'm afraid you'll have to eat with the crew—all the dining-rooms are being used as sets. And I'd better mention now that this lounge is the only room available to you for boozing and socialising. All other rooms in the Manor are strictly out of bounds—Art Director's orders.'

'Speaking of directors and orders,' Darren Williams asked from the depth of his chair, 'where is the great man himself? Skulking in his room, in search of inspiration?'

Lindsey ignored the sulky petulance. 'Still in London, I guess. And I wouldn't wait up for him. He won't get here much before dawn.'

'You mean I'm supposed to go on set cold, with no preliminary talks with the director?' the star exclaimed angrily. 'This is a bit much, you know! I hardly know what part I'm supposed to play . . .'

'I'm sorry,' Lindsey answered sweetly, obviously not very impressed either by him or his fame. 'I'm sure you'll have plenty time to talk to him tomorrow, and meanwhile, why don't you read the script?'

'Insufferable cow!' Darren spat when Lindsey was gone. 'What happened to Nick's old assistant? He was charming . . .'

'Gone on to better things, friend,' Francis announced, his voice thick with drink. 'He's now directing his own film.'

'Oh, really? Who's in it?' The professional gossip diverted the actor's aroused wrath and kept him going all the way to the kitchen and dinner.

It was after ten when Jo returned to her room. Sounds of a rowdy, high-spirited party drifted in through the open windows. The production crew were obviously celebrating their first night on location in the staff cottages. She could hear bursts of laughter, the odd coarse if goodnatured curse, and the tinny hammering of an old piano playing 'Show Me the Way to go Home'. I'll ask Lindsey to introduce me to the rest of the crew, she decided. If the few she had already met were anything to go by, they were a friendly, down-to-earth lot, nearer her age and not as steeped in showbiz gossip and endless moanings about contracts, fees and schedules as were the actors with whom she had spent the evening. Among the cast, she felt too young and inexperienced. Most of their jokes had passed over her head, and she became very tired of Darren's repeated efforts at playing the seductive lover with her. She had been pestered at school often enough by would-be Casanovas and had learnt to keep them at arm's length without arousing too much animosity, so she wasn't unduly worried about him, but she would have preferred not to be bothered by similar tedious advances on her first film.

Reluctantly, she realised that her slight discontent had to do with the fact that Nicholas Hayward was missing all evening. She hated to admit that she had been waiting impatiently to see him again.

Oh, forget it, she decided. And to hell with Nick of the past and with Nicholas Hayward of the present. She was going to enjoy her first film whether he liked it or not. So what if he was a dictator, a slavedriver? His films, each and every one of them, were great and had launched many young actors on very successful careers. She was going to use him just as he meant to use her and as he had used her mother before her.

Each man to his own, she chuckled out loud. I can be as coldbloodedly calculating as you, Mr Hayward!

She was arranging her toilet things in the luxurious ivory bathroom when the sound of loud voices drifted in from the door which connected it to the next room: a high-pitched angry feminine squeal and Lindsey's American staccato.

'What do you mean, share a bathroom? Share with whom? The chief electrician? Or perhaps that's too good for me . . . how about the catering chap?'

'It's Josephine Montague . . . she's the only other regular girl on the cast, and I'm sure she'll be careful not to—'

'I don't care if it's Princess Diana. I won't share a bathroom with anyone!' Andrea Burton's voice rose to a strident pitch. 'You either get me another room or get the little fool to use the bath in the hall!'

'I don't think that's possible, Miss Burton.'

'Then make it possible. Now get out! I had a ghastly flight and I'm still jet-lagged, so will you please make sure I'm not disturbed till dinner?'

Jo giggled to herself. Stars were supposed to have nasty tempers and felt obliged to throw a tantrum now and then. Though her mother had never felt the need to demonstrate her status by what she considered to be a silly and tiring waste of energy.

She had no intention of taking a bath, but out of mischief, she turned the taps full blast, and as she expected, the bathroom door began to shudder under an attack of furious knocks. 'Hey, you there . . . can you hear me?' Jo remained silent. 'I say, do you mind turning those taps off for a second?'

She let the water run for a few seconds more and then turned them off and said innocently: 'Yes?'

'Are you going to be there long?'

'Oh, ten minutes . . . I'll try to hurry up,' Jo called back.

'I'm tired,' the voice went on, trying to curb its surliness. 'I must freshen up after the flight. Would you mind letting me use the bathroom before you?'

'Oh, I'm terribly sorry,' Jo answered, 'but I'm already in the tub.' She ran her hand in the shallow water to simulate the sound of a splashing body.

'You're lying!' Andrea's voice became strident again and then she stormed in.

Jo knew she was staring, but she couldn't help herself. Andrea Burton was beautiful. Even with her hair ruffled and the obvious signs of a transatlantic flight, she was stunning. Her small, delicate body was sheathed in beautifully cut trousers and an Yves St Laurent silk blouse Jo had seen in last week's *Vogue*. Its deep blue shade enhanced the star's violet eyes and the smooth, creamy skin which glowed under a cascade of straight, long blue-black hair. She had no make-up on, allowing her natural beauty to speak for itself.

'I knew it!' the hard strident voice broke the spell of

the incredible beauty. 'You aren't even undressed, you little—'

'Hello,' Jo said pleasantly. 'You must be Andrea Burton.'

For a moment they stared at each other, the younger girl looking calm and polite, the other shooting darts of instant dislike. And then a slow, sweet smile dispelled the angry frown and Jo braced herself for an attack of irresistible charm:

'Sorry I lost my temper, darling . . . but I'm so utterly exhausted. You're Jo Montague, of course . . .' Her laughter was friendly and warm, so very different from the recent ugly, strident voice. 'I was so curious to meet Emma Montague's daughter; she used to be my idol, you know . . . I was heartbroken when I heard about the way Nick's been treating her. Isn't he a beast sometimes?' Prettily, her hand flew to her mouth as she gave a little gasp: 'Oops, I forgot! Nick told me he wanted to keep your mother's name out of this.'

'Did he?' Jo's face didn't reflect that pain inflicted by the words. She was sure it wasn't a slip of the tongue. There was a taunting, cruel intention behind it. 'In that case, perhaps you'd better not repeat it in front of anyone else.'

'Of course not, sweetie, I promise never to breathe another word. And you won't tell on me to Nick, will you? He'll be so angry. He gets so unreasonably furious when his orders are not obeyed to the letter. You know how he is . . .'

The purring voice was implying very carefully that although Jo might have known him since childhood, it was she, Andrea, who now held him in the palm of her soft little hand.

'I don't really,' Jo answered mildly. 'I've never work-ed with Mr Hayward before. This is my first film, you see.' And unable to curb a pang of unreasonable jealousy, she walked out of the bathroom, apologising coldly: 'I'd better let you take your bath now, Miss Burton. Goodnight.'

There was a slight pause and then she could hear the woman storm back to her own room and shout at Lindsey, who had obviously been waiting there all the time, enjoying the catty encounter. 'That's it! I'm not staying in this room another moment. You get me another room, or I'm leaving!' Lindsey was trying to say something in a low voice, but was interrupted again. 'I don't care . . . Give me Theodore's room, or Nick's. I'm not staying with that little minx next door!'

The slamming of the distant hall door put an end to the interlude.

Leaving the window open, Jo got out of her clothes, threw her T-shirt on and crawled into the large four-poster bed. She fell asleep immediately, the cool night air caressing her cheeks.

She woke up suddenly, her sleep broken by the faint but nerve-racking sound of dripping water. Either she or her reluctant bathmate had neglected to turn off the taps properly, she deduced. The monotonous, rhythmic drip made her think of the old Chinese water torture. Irrit-ated, she threw the covers off and groped her way in the dark towards the offending noise, reluctant to expel the last shreds of sleep by switching on the lights.

A sudden, harsh shift of neon light hit her as she opened the bathroom door. With her eyes shut tightly against it, she stumbled in the direction of the tub, knocked her knees painfully against the hard rim and stretched a hand to find the dripping tap.

Her stomach rose to her throat, choking a scream. Instead of the hard cold metal, her hand encountered the luxuriant warm texture of human hair. After a second of paralysed terror, she managed to open her eyes and found herself gazing into a pair of sparkling blue eyes, which crinkled at her with a teasing, good-humoured familiarity.

'Nicky!' she whispered hoarsely when she finally found her voice.

'Hi, Jo,' he said in his light, lazy voice.

Bent as she still was, her hand hovering over his head in an attempt to reach the tap, her face was hardly two inches away from his. 'Oh, dear,' she stammered, 'I—I didn't know . . . I mean, I thought—'

'You didn't expect to find me here, is that what you're trying to tell me?' Jo could only nod. 'Last-minute change. Andrea was threatening to fly back to the States if she didn't get a room with her own bathroom, and I quite liked the idea of sharing a bathroom with you again. After all, we are quite old hands at it, aren't we?' He was referring to his frequent visits to her parents' home: his usual room was separated from her nursery by a shared bathroom. 'And I suppose I should be grateful to you. I must have dozed off. I might have drowned if you hadn't walked in here and woken me up. The water is freezing!'

Gently pushing her head away, he sat up. Her stunned gaze was fixed on the rippling muscles of his broad, smooth back as he bent forward to pull out the plug and let some cold water out before he reached for the hot-water tap to warm up the cooling bath.

He seemed utterly unperturbed by Jo's presence, as he settled back, to relax in the hot water. 'Isn't it nice, honey? Us meeting like that again?' He asked conversationally. 'How are you?'

'Oh, fine, thank you,' she answered politely. 'And you?'

'Oh, I'm fine too, Joey. Tired but fine.' She couldn't believe that she was actually conducting polite small-talk with a naked man, with Nick. She was all too painfully aware of the gleaming, powerful shape of his broad shoulders, the lean, hard golden chest submerged in the water. Involuntarily, her eyes followed the tufts of golden hair as they tapered down the centre towards the flat stomach and—With a gasp, she averted her shocked gaze and frantically tried to take refuge in something more neutral, only to be assaulted by the smiling mockery of Nick's gaze. It held her a prisoner for a long moment and then it left her to wander slowly down her own body, hidden behind the soft cotton T-shirt.

'Still wearing a man's T-shirt to bed, I see?' he murmured. 'I could swear it's the one I gave you myself. Is it?' His arm shot out of the water and squeezed the soft, often-laundered material which hardly hid the rounded curves of her slim hips. 'Come and sit down,' he invited, his arm pulling her by the T-shirt towards him. 'I feel like a midnight chat.'

Like a trapped mouse, her eyes skipped away from his hand on her stomach and found relative shelter in the gold chain around the strong, tanned column of his neck. It had been her Christmas present to him some seven years ago. For all the memories it brought back, it seemed the only harmless item on his body.

'You're naked,' she reminded him, dumbly.

'So I believe, honey. But since you've been studying me keenly for the last five minutes, there's nothing more I can hide from you.' His smile was amused, teasing, painfully familiar. He began to chuckle. 'Don't look so petrified, Jo!'

'I am not petrified,' Jo stammered.

Nicholas ignored her protest. 'Isn't it funny? Here we are again, in the bathroom, with me inside and you out. How would you like to join me? You're hardly eleven years old now, but I'm sure the tub is large enough to hold you, even now.' His hand tightened around her waist as he tried to pull her into the water. The touch of the strong, wet hand made her jump with an irrepressible quiver.

'I . . . I'd better go back to my room,' she managed to announce, feebly trying to free herself from his unyielding hold.

'Oh, no, don't. We won't have many chances of nice quiet chats once we begin shooting, Jo. Tell you what . . . why don't you turn off the light, and then you won't be able to see even the whites of my eyes.'

Like a puppet without a will of her own, she obeyed him. He was right. The total darkness brought immediate relief.

'Here, Jo, come and sit on the rim, like you used to. Here's my hand . . .'

Jo stepped forward and again felt his wet hand which inadvertently met her breasts through the flimsy fabric of the T-shirt. The touch was electrifying, forcing both her hands to come up in an attempt to tear it away. But instead of wrenching herself free, her fingers seemed to obey their own need, and kept clinging to his strong sinewy hand.

'That's better.' He pulled her down until she was sitting on the wet tub, her two hands still holding on to his. 'I've missed our nightly chats, you know.'

She forgot where she was, engulfed by a protective blanket of darkness, sustained only by his voice and by the touch of his hand in hers. 'Oh, Nicky, I missed you too . . . I missed you so much!' A broken whisper let out all the bewilderment and yearnings which she had been trying so hard to repress ever since that night on the Corfu beach.

He wasn't really listening to her. 'Did you, Joey?' he murmured, his slow, lazy voice caressing her. His free hand was tracing the line of her cheeks, reaching for her mouth and then sliding down towards her neck.

In the still darkness, she could hear the quickening of his shallow breathing as the touch of his roaming hands began to change, almost imperceptively, becoming more insistent, less absentminded. A small groan escaped her lips as she became aware of an aching sweetness flowing. His chuckle was a little breathless. 'And to think that they all had to sweat blood to get me to agree to have you on my set,' he mumbled. His voice reminded her suddenly of the way he had spoken to her in Corfu when he thought she was Nadia, his girl-friend. 'Why, Josephine Montague, I'm beginning to think this production is going to be great fun for both of us. You seem almost grown up . . . Are you?'

'Am I what?' she asked, bemused and increasingly disturbed by the tone of his voice and his odd enigmatic remark. It felt as if he had forgotten who she was and was confusing her with his numerous easily discarded girl-friends.

'Grown up?'

'Yes,' she answered, then retreated. 'No . . . I don't know. My friends tell me I'm not, but I feel—' she stopped abruptly, realising in a flash that he was referring to her experience with men. Blushing in the darkness, she couldn't bring herself to tell this seductive stranger that no man had ever touched her, except he himself. Desperately, she pulled herself away and tried to remind him who she was. 'Oh, Nicky, why did you keep away all this time?'

'I was busy,' he answered, a little abruptly. 'And anyway, I did come back. I came to see your first public appearance.' Years ago he had given her his oath that he would be present at her first night, even if he had to come all the way from the North Pole for it.

'I didn't see you,' she complained. 'You should have come backstage after the show and told me whether you liked it.'

'I invited you to audition for me instead,' he muttered. The impatience was undisguised now. He was obviously not very interested in talking to her right now. The water splashed softly as he raised himself slightly and drew her unresisting body to his wet, hard chest. The soft warm breath of his mouth teased her hair. 'Anyway, Jo honey, you probably would have slammed kicked me in the shins as you almost did during your audition. After all, you were supposed to hate me for what I've done to Emma—'

Nick halted. Jo hadn't moved, but he immediately sensed that he had shattered the dreamlike scene. 'Oh, boy . . .' he cursed softly, 'that certainly was the wrong thing to say right now!'

As if catapulated by a cannon, Jo found herself back at the bathroom door, free of his stroking hands. 'You bet it was, you . . . you bastard!' Her lips pronounced the rarely used word as if to strengthen the sudden blaze of animosity which Emma's name had rekindled.

He laughed. 'Well, well, well . . . such words, Jo! I'm surprised at you. You used to be such a polite little girl . .'

As if to assert that she was no longer entrapped by the memory of her yearnings, she switched on the light, her eyes blinded by hatred and the old shame of humiliation.

'God, Jo,' he said, no longer amused, 'you don't really hold me responsible for Emma's retirement, do you?'

She gaped at him, in furious amazement. 'You want me to answer that?'

Nicholas relapsed into silence. Hate emanated from her like an electric current.

'Don't you think you should know the facts before you throw an accusation like that in my face?' he said finally, an odd hint of curiosity in his voice.

'Can you deny it? Can you deny the fact that you fired Emma in order to put your latest girl-friend in her place?' The image of Andrea Burton's lovely, cruel face flashed before her eyes.

'My girl-friend?' In spite of her blinding fury she couldn't ignore the note of amazement. 'Is that what you think I did?'

'I don't think . . . I know!'

To her disgust, Nick responded with a bark of hard, cold laughter. 'All right, then, let's leave it at that.'

His indifferent admission threw her into a momentary confusion. 'So it's true?'

'If that's what you want to believe, why not? But don't expect me to justify myself. Both your mother and I have been telling you for years that there's no place for personal feelings when it comes to the quality of the end product.'

'What end product?' she gasped. 'Another Nicholas Hayward masterpiece? Is it worth ruining the career of your best friend, my mother . . . after all she'd done for you?'

'I couldn't ruin your mother's career even if I wanted to, you idiot. She's far too great an actress to suffer from one single decision . . . oh, all right, one whim of a ruthless director.'

'I'm glad you know that!' Jo hissed.

Nick said nothing for a moment. 'I wonder what happened to the cuddly little girl who found it so easy to trust me,' he said at last, sounding genuinely curious.

'You killed her!' she spat.

'I did?' he asked, amazed, underlining the personal pronoun. 'What have I done?'

She didn't bother to answer. In one single stride she was back in her room, the door to the bathroom shut behind her back.

Yet she remained glued to her place, listening to the sound of splashing water as he got out of the bath. The silence stretched endlessly. For a moment she thought that he had retired to his room and she felt the pang of bitter disappointment.

'It's going to be somewhat difficult working with such a wall of fury between us,' his quiet voice came from behind the door, hardly muffled by the wooden barrier. 'I warn you, Jo. I won't stand for any hysterical tantrums on set, do you understand that?'

'Oh, God forbid!' she almost screamed back at him. 'I wouldn't dare give you any trouble, sir. I know my place. You're the boss, I'm nothing but an actress!'

'Good,' he said. 'And as your boss I would be quite pleased if you released all that unsuspected fire and fury in front of the cameras instead of at me.'

'Yes, Mr Hayward,' she called back.

'Nicholas,' he reminded her. 'Or Nick. No one calls me Mr Hayward on set. And incidentally, in future I expect you to spend your nights in bed, and asleep. I don't want you looking worn out on set. So please, no more midnight visits, either to my room or anyone else's.'

'I didn't—' she started to protest furiously.

'Goodnight, Jo.'

In helpless rage, she attacked the door and turned the key firmly. 'Oh, you don't need to take these precautions with me, honey. I rarely indulge in that kind of activity while shooting. Only when strongly tempted . . . and believe me, I don't relish tiring myself out with a repeat performance of such tantrums again.' Then, as if on second thoughts, he added: 'Still, it would be a good idea if you locked your hall door. Other guys won't share my views on the matter, and you do look rather appetising!'

She was struggling with the key, trying to open the door and attack him physically, but by the time she managed to wrest it open, he was gone.

Things had certainly changed between them, she realised as she stormed back into her bed. Three years ago Nick had threatened to thrash her for trying to seduce him, as he had put it then. She cringed as she remembered the shame and misery she had suffered all these years, for having cheapened herself so abysmally in front of him. Well, he definitely had no such scruples now. Whatever concern he had had for her as an adolescent, he now regarded her as just another young, greedy actress: senseless putty in his hands by daytime and a possible temporary entertainment by night. He was quite ready to end that touching bathroom reunion in either his or her bed.

To her shame, she couldn't pretend that the prospect was altogether repulsive to her. On the contrary. Her body, mocking her furious moral indignation, gave a delicious shiver as it remembered the exploring, sensuous touch of his wet hands and the vision of his naked golden body in the water.

'To hell with you!' Nick Hayward, she exploded out loud. 'You'll have to rely on Andrea for this kind of service. I'm damned if I'll let you drag me into that old game of location musical beds!' And comforted by the strength of her resolution, she instantly fell asleep.

CHAPTER FOUR

'FOR God's sake, Jo, don't try to act! Just stand still and let the camera do the rest.'

Jo blinked at the blaring spotlights, shut her mouth tight so as not to explode in a curse and made her body go stiff, waiting rigidly for the burring sound of the camera to be interrupted by Nicholas Hayward's call of 'Cut!' She had been doing the same shot now for the fourth time, but the great genius was still dissatisfied.

Filming, she had found out, was no child's game . . . and far from an adult's idea of fun. The phone had woken her up at half past five and Lindsey, on the other end, informed her cheerfully that the make-up girl was ready for her.

At seven she was taken to the forest on the edge of the estate where she was met by an army of sleepy-eyed grips, gaffers and other seasoned technicians. The only cheerful, widely awake smile was offered her by Peter, already busy behind the large, impressive camera.

'Morning, Jo. What a nice face to see first thing in the morning!' he had greeted her as if he had been awake for hours. 'I think you and I are going to make beautiful music together . . . if this lady here,' he pointed lovingly at the camera, 'if this lady here doesn't dig her heels in. One never knows which face she likes and which she rejects. But judging from your screen test, I would say you belong with the chosen few. Great eyes and fantastic bone structure . . . and I'm going to do a lot with that hair of yours.'

By eight o'clock, there was still no sign of Nicholas Hayward.

'So why did I have to be up and ready at six-thirty?' she asked Peter.

'Don't ask me, love. That's the way we play the game. Tradition, I guess.'

'By the time we start, my costume will be all creased and dirty,' she complained.

'Your costume?' Peter burst out laughing. 'Didn't they tell you that by the end of the day this lovely dress of yours will be torn to shreds?'

'*Why?*' she shrieked. It was a lovingly made sprigged muslin gown, high-waisted, with a wide blue sash and small puffed sleeves. With her hair gathered into long, tight curls, a few wisps falling softly over her forehead, she looked exactly what she was supposed to be: a well-brought-up fifteen-year-old girl in 1815.

'We're shooting one of the final scenes . . . the one in which you try and drown yourself in the lake, before Sir John stops you. Scenes 163 and 164.'

Jo quickly opened her script, looking for the scene number. The whole action was described in one short paragraph. There were no spoken lines, but there was enough in that paragraph to throw her into panic.

'You mean I'm supposed to throw myself into the lake today?'

'No, not today,' Nicholas Hayward, cool and relaxed and utterly impersonal, answered her from behind. 'You'll need warming up before we cool you in the freezing water.' Turning away, he addressed the waiting crew. 'Sorry about the delay . . . problems with

Andrea's contract. We'll have to go twice as fast to catch up with lost time.'

He was wearing jeans and a large black fisherman's sweater, which accentuated his slim hips and broad shoulders. His fair hair looked like pale gold in the bright April morning sun.

He stood looking down at her, his eyes taking in her costume, hair and make-up, and she forced herself to stand still and take his scrutiny unflinchingly. But then, suddenly, his hand shot out, and Jo recoiled involuntarily as it descended on her low-cut dress and pulled it up, so as to cover her slightly exposed breasts.

'That won't do,' he said to the wardrobe woman who was hovering anxiously beside Jo. 'It's far too low. Can you do something about it?'

For a few moments she became the centre of attention. The wardrobe lady, the make-up girl, even Peter and the chief electrician, were buzzing around her like angry wasps, moving her about, touching up her make-up, pulling at her dress. She had no idea what was expected of her, so she just stood there and revelled in the strange thrill of it.

But the excitement was very shortlived. She was made to stand there for half an hour, feeling awkward and superfluous in the midst of the frantic activity around her. Her legs were beginning to ache and her neck muscles felt sore with tension. This certainly was a far cry from her fantasies about the glamour of film-making!

'Right, Jo,' she jumped as Nicholas Hayward suddenly materialised beside her, 'we'll start with a few simple shots; initiate you gently, so to speak. I want you to stand exactly where you are and just . . .' his eyes were boring straight into hers, serious, intent, dedicated.

'Don't stand there like a rigid pole, honey. Let your shoulders relax . . .' he gave a slight push. 'That's better. Now, the rest is very simple. All I want you to do, for starters, is to stand still and when I call your name, turn your head towards me . . . only your head, that's right . . . and look at my hand, there.' His hand was raised a little above his head and she obeyed him, raising her eyes to it, dumbly. 'Yes, like that—and keep looking until I tell you to stop.' His cold face suddenly broke in a warm smile. 'That's great, honey. Do you think you can remember that?'

'Yes,' she said shortly, feeling like a dumb pet. 'But—'

'But what?' the sharp tone seemed to warn her not to question his orders.

'Well, I mean . . . is that all? Just turn and look?'

'If you do that much, honey, I'll be more than pleased.'

'Sorry,' she mumbled.

'That's quite all right,' he said politely. 'Ready?' Jo nodded, shaking inwardly but keeping a straight, cool face. 'Well then, let's go. Camera?' he called towards Peter.

'Ready!' Peter called back, sounding like a peddler in the market.

'Clapper?' Nicholas suggested gently.

Someone ran in front of her, pushed the black wooden clapper-board in front of her nose and disappeared.

'Action!'

It took her a second to identify the burring noise as the camera coming alive. Taken aback, she turned to look at it.

'Cut!'

Everything came to a standstill.

'Damn it, Jo!' Nicholas was towering over her. 'Don't—I repeat—don't ever stare at the camera! You ought to know that much. You've visited your mother and me on set often enough!'

'I'm sorry,' she stammered, blushing furiously. 'I wasn't ready for—'

'But I said—' he stopped and then groaned softly. 'Sorry, honey. I keep forgetting this is your first shot.' She smiled, grateful for this tiny show of understanding. 'This is unforgivable,' he continued, turning to the crew. 'We should have done something to celebrate this. Lindsey!' The tiny assistant materialised beside him, looking slight and elfish in her baggy khaki trousers and her huge sweat-shirt. 'Is there any champagne on set?'

'No, Nick . . . sorry. Only beer.'

'Pity,' he sounded genuinely sorry. 'But it'll have to do.'

In a few moments every member of the crew was holding a beer can or a small soft drink bottle, Jo herself included. Nicholas was holding her free hand, waiting for Lindsey to finish distributing the drinks.

'Now,' he said to the crew, 'let me introduce you to Jo Montague . . . . this is her first film and we're about to shoot her first shot. So what do we do to that?'

Her hand, held tightly in his, felt secure and protected. For a moment she forgot he was her enemy. The crew was singing 'For she's a jolly good fellow' in good-humoured mockery, ending with the traditional 'Hip-hip-hooray!' and suddenly she was swept off her feet, scooped into Nick's strong, sinewy arms and thrown into the air.

When she felt the ground under her feet again, everyone applauded, drank deeply from the beer cans and the ceremony was over, as she gathered from Nick's dry voice. 'That's it, Jo,' he said dryly. There was no trace of the jocular affection he had shown a moment ago. 'Now, shall we try again? And if I catch you staring at the camera once more, I'll skin you! Got that?'

She was hardly allowed to do anything. He stopped her again before she even turned her head.

'I don't want any expression on that face of yours, Jo,' he said dryly. 'Just obey my orders. Don't give me any extra. You'll have a chance to earn your fee later on.'

'I wasn't trying to show any expression,' she protested after the third aborted effort. 'I don't understand what you want of me.'

'Just wipe your face clean . . . look dumb . . . look like you're asleep. Anything. Only don't try to act, for God's sake!'

She had to repeat the same shot four times, never understanding what was wrong with the one before, but soon realising that it was better not to ask questions. As Nicholas led her firmly but securely through relatively simple still shots into more complex ones, she learnt to follow his orders to the letter, demanding no explanations. After an hour she felt as if she had been standing in front of the camera for days, feeling confident and experienced.

'Cut,' Nicholas called finally, sounding content. 'Was that all right for you, Peter?'

'Absolutely. Couldn't be better.'

'You see?' Nicholas turned back to her. 'That wasn't too difficult, was it?'

'No,' Jo agreed calmly. 'Can we start working now, or do you think I need a few more initiating exercises?'

'You'll be fine now, honey,' he answered, giving her a

familiar conspiratorial smile. 'You're almost a pro. We'll print the last one, Lindsey,' he instructed the assistant. 'Next shot, everybody.'

That was the last personal exchange between them for many days to come. And Jo almost welcomed the mantle of professional impersonality which was now thrown over her relationship with Nick. The see-saw pendulum of his attitude, veering from cold, harsh criticism to friendly, almost old-time affection, left her mentally and emotionally drained. The physical exhaustion to which Nick exposed her now was almost easy in comparison. He made her stand for hours, doing nothing but obeying silly orders like moving an arm, looking pensive, looking scared . . . then she was told to run across the green lawns, into the forest . . . trip, fall, pick herself up, making sure the hem of her dress got torn in the process. As Peter had predicted, by midday her dress was a soiled rag, her hair free of its tidy curls and her make-up smeared with mud and genuine tears.

She was allowed half an hour lunch-break, which was delicious even if served in a lunch-box, and then Darren and Francis joined her on set.

Now, to top it all, she had to cope with Darren's endless approaches. The man simply refused to leave her side. Whether they were doing a scene together or just standing idly while everyone else was preparing for the next, he kept pushing her hair back, rearranging her torn dress over her shoulders, resting a brotherly arm on her back as if she hadn't had enough trouble supporting her own weight. Twice she felt the blush cover her face as Nicholas commented on her growing intimacy with his dashing leading man.

'Do you mind leaving your loving explorations for

another time?' he drawled lazily at Darren, whose hands were busily straying up and down Jo's back. 'I want her fresh and eager for your amorous hands when the time comes, in front of the camera . . . don't waste it on her now, okay?'

And once more, when, angrily and utterly exhausted by Darren's insistence, she pushed his hand away from her hip, causing him to stumble: 'Please, Jo . . . I promise you many opportunities to lay your hands on him. Let go for now . . . we're wasting valuable daylight hours.'

'I didn't lay hands on him!' she exploded, her voice rising.

'Didn't you? Well, just make sure you keep it that way, then.'

She was quite numb when she heard Nicholas announce the final shot. It was past six.

'All right, everybody,' Lindsey took over. 'You can pack up. Dinner's in the kitchen in five minutes.'

'Tired, love?' Francis Blakely let her lean against him as he led her towards the warm house and badly needed dinner.

'Fed up,' she corrected him. 'I'm afraid that by the time we start shooting real scenes, I won't be able to open my mouth, let alone utter a line with any conviction!'

'Oh, you will, darling, you will. As much as I abhor Nick's initiation methods, he does have a point. It's always the same working with him. He warms his actors up by bullying them, exhausting them physically, provoking their anger, and then starts using them for real, as intelligent, reliable partners. It never fails.' He smiled sideways at the soiled, untidy girl who was limping beside him. 'You'll hate him like poison for the next few days, but mark my words, darling . . . the moment you'll do your first honest to goodness acting scene, you'll worship him.' Something in Jo's expression made him stop and look at her thoughtfully. 'Look, Jo, it's none of my business, of course, but I wouldn't hold a grudge against him because of your mother. These are professional hazards, you know.'

'So you know about it?' Jo looked at him. 'Well, maybe when I'm forty I'll be numb enough to forget professional hazards, as you call it. Right now, I can't. This part was an offer I couldn't refuse, but once I'm launched, I'll never work with Nicholas Hayward again. Never!'

Francis sighed. 'You'll change your mind one day. Still, my dear, hating him as you do right now is preferable to falling in love with him.' He turned to her, speaking intently. 'Now this is a real professional hazard. Just take my advice, Jo. Whatever you do, don't let his occasional bouts of charm fool you. If you care anything for your peace of mind, don't fall for him.'

Jo stopped dead. 'What makes you think I'm likely to? I've only just told you I hate his guts!'

'They all say that after the first day, love . . . and then they all succumb. So just take my word for it. He's deadly. Leave him to Andrea and her kind . . . they can deal with it. Not you.'

Most of the crew was already seated around the long oak table in the vast kitchen, devouring the delicious meal which had been prepared by the hotel chef. Jo was still wearing her torn, soiled dress, but she did manage to wash the make-up and the mud off her hands and face.

Trying to avoid Darren, she found an empty chair at

the less crowded end of the table. She noticed that Francis, like herself, was keeping away from the other actors, though she sensed that his objection was primarily to Andrea, who was already into her second course, looking fresh and breathtakingly beautiful in a deceptively simple Givenchy T-shirt and face clean of any artificial enchancement.

'Well, my love,' she graciously singled Jo out, calling from the far end of the table, 'how did you enjoy your first day?'

'It was . . .' Jo, hesitated and then decided to answer truthfully, 'it was hell. But I'll live.'

'I'm sure you will, darling,' Andrea purred, her voice sweet and solicitous. 'Where is Nick?'

'Going over tomorrow's schedule with Peter,' Francis answered for Jo. 'Don't worry, Andie . . . he'll soon be here to pay his respects to you.' The veiled hostility was quite unsettling, especially from a kind and sensitive man like Francis Blakely.

'Oh, lovely,' Andrea ignored the barb. 'I do hope he's going to start on me tomorrow . . . I'm supposed to be back in Hollywood by Sunday and Nick knows he ought to arrange his working schedule to fit in with mine. I wonder,' she threw Francis a defiant, mocking glance, 'I wonder if he's going to do my bedroom scene with you tomorrow.' Jo remembered one scene in which Helena/Andrea was tantalising her thoroughly disgusted husband, trying to arouse his dead passion and change his mind about divorcing her after her last infidelity.

'Not if the good weather holds,' Francis answered dryly. 'Nick wants to do all the exteriors first.'

'How boring,' Andrea murmured.

'Are you that keen to strip again?' Francis shot at her.

'I thought you'd had enough of that after your last film. You were hardly ever clothed in it.'

'I never object to stripping if the script and the part call for it,' she said primly. Jo chuckled inwardly at the trite, universal justification of every actress in the profession. 'And I'm not at all keen on it. I find I can be just as effectively seductive with all my clothes on.'

Darren, his face buried in the hot, steaming soup, stopped for a second to look up: 'Don't tell Jo that, Andie,' he drawled. 'She hasn't had her baptism of fire yet . . .' and he chuckled at his own joke.

'What . . . what do you mean?' Jo broke the silence which followed his remark.

'Nothing,' Darren sniggered. 'Nothing.'

Jo gulped. There was nothing in the script to indicate that she was required to strip. She had several love scenes which already worried her a lot, especially since they had mostly to do with Darren, whom she was beginning to find utterly repulsive. To imagine herself naked, or even half naked, in his arms, in front of two dozen crew members, studied vigorously by the camera and exposed to Nick's cold eyes, was something she hadn't bargained for.

Too engrossed in her horrified suspicions, she hadn't noticed that the two empty chairs on her left and her right had been claimed by Peter and Nicholas. His light, lazy voice came to her as an unsettling surprise. 'Well, Josephine Montague, had a good day?'

'Yes, thank you,' she answered, her voice hoarse.

'Is that all? Didn't you find it tiring? Boring? Repetitious?' His lazy mockery infuriated her.

'That too, but I can take it.'

'Good, because it's only the beginning, honey. You're

about to be plunged into the real stuff. I hope you know your lines.'

'I do . . .' she snapped.

'How can you be so sure? You don't even know what scenes I'm thinking of doing first.'

'I know the whole script by heart!' She was trembling with penned-up rage.

'Good girl! We'll put you to the test tomorrow.'

'I thought you were going to do my exteriors tomorrow,' Andrea interrupted. There was the slight note of whining sulkiness in her tone.

'So I am . . . I meant Wednesday, of course.' Unceremoniously, he turned his back on Jo and attended to Andrea, his voice softening noticeably. 'We've arranged the schedule so that you could leave here on Friday. But I still want you back towards the end of the shooting . . . for the crowd scenes.'

'That's all right, darling,' the star smiled. 'I've arranged to have the whole of May free, so that I could even give myself a holiday once the film is over.' Watching Jo from the corner of her eye, Andrea let show the real state of affairs between her and the director. 'We'll both need it, darling.'

'I guess so,' Nicholas said coldly.

Feeling slightly sick, Jo forced herself to eat her dinner, deaf to the lively conversation around the table. The moment she saw that Nick was once again absorbed in a technical discussion with two of the crew, she turned to Peter, who was sitting quietly on her left. 'Peter, does he really want me to appear . . . I mean, will there be nude scenes in the film?'

Peter looked a bit stunned. 'Nude scenes? Not that I know of. Why?'

'Well, Darren said that—' She stopped as she realised that the actor was looking at her from across the table, obviously aware of her turbulence.

'Nick,' he called out, in mock curiosity, 'can you think of any way of shooting a bedroom love scene other than in the nude?'

'I can,' answered the director, not very interested in the question. 'But I don't see why. Any special reason for asking that, Darren?'

'Well, I seem to remember one specific love scene between Gilbert and Melissa, in her bedroom . . .'

Nicholas turned his pensive blue gaze on Jo. 'Does that bother you, Jo?'

'Yes,' she admitted, whispering.

'We'll cross that bridge when we come to it,' he dismissed her. 'Meanwhile, just concentrate on the scenes at hand.' The blue eyes narrowed as if in indifferent contempt. 'There are other aspects to this film beside lovemaking, you know.'

'Don't worry about it, Jo,' whispered Peter when Nicholas diverted his attention back to Francis. 'Nick doesn't go for explicit nudity, and if he does, he never uses his leading actress to do so. We usually use an understudy to stand in—or rather lie in for her.'

His feeble attempt to amuse her failed. 'I'll still have to str—' she cleared her throat. 'I'll have to take my clothes off, won't I?'

'I doubt it, knowing Nick's style. But even so, you'll see it's quite harmless. None of us will ogle you. We'll be far too busy doing our jobs.'

'Anything wrong, Jo?' Andrea called to her, in a falsely concerned voice. 'You look so tired.'

'I'm fine, thank you.'

'Don't let us keep you, darling,' Andrea encouraged her sweetly. 'You must be exhausted. Why not go upstairs and soak in a nice hot bath?'

Perhaps it was her imagination, but Jo was sure the sweetly smiling lips were mocking her. She imagined she saw a glance pass between the star and Nicholas, as if in a shared joke. She was sure he had told her about their nocturnal meeting the night before. Her head reeled as the memory of that long, powerful yet lithe body invaded her mind. She could see it suddenly intertwined with that of Andrea and she choked on the fruit she was munching.

'Here, drink this,' Nicholas was thumping her back vigorously, his other hand forcing a glass of water into her hand.

'Thank you,' she managed at last and stood up. 'I think I will have an early night. Will you excuse me?' and with a shaky smile at Peter and Francis she managed to escape from the hot kitchen.

'Lovely manners, don't you think?' Andrea's remark followed her to the corridor. 'But then you would expect no less from Emma Montague's daughter, would you?'

'You're a bitch, Andrea.' Francis's well-trained, mellow voice was the last thing she heard.

In her room, she got out of the torn dress and was about to go into the bathroom for her bath when her eyes caught the reflection of her naked body in the large mirror. Without vanity, she was quite aware that it was a very beautiful form, slim, long-limbed, with small firm breasts and gently curving hips. She tried to imagine herself as she was now, naked except for her flimsy bikini briefs, in front of a crew, feeling Nicholas Hayward's icy blue eyes scan her in that hateful impersonal manner, and immediately the panic she had felt before, at the kitchen table, rose to the surface.

She was no prude. There were hundreds of good, much admired actresses who were quite ready to appear naked in a film or on stage if they were convinced the part demanded it. But she had neither the confidence nor the temperament to carry such a thing through. It was no use, she decided. She would have to refuse, even if it meant a breach of contract. 'I won't, then,' she said out loud, and stepped into the hot bath.

A little after midnight someone knocked on her door. It was so soft that for a moment she thought she had imagined it, but soon it was repeated and before she could ask who it was, the door opened and Darren, in a blue Dior dressing-gown, crept in. 'Oh, good,' he whispered, 'you're still awake.'

'Oh, damn you, Darren!' she exploded, not caring if she was heard in the next room. 'Can't you leave me alone?'

'I thought you might like to go over our scenes together,' he whispered, trying to look innocent. 'I mean, you seemed a little unsure of yourself today, and I don't mind giving you some coaching before you face His Eminence again.' He was coming nearer as he was talking and by the end of the speech, he settled on the edge of her bed.

'Thanks, but I've had enough of both of you for one day. Please go away, Darren.'

'All right, so let's just chat . . .'

'No . . . I want to sleep.'

'Just a few moments, Jo. Honestly.'

'No!' Jo's voice rose to a squeal. 'I don't want you

here. I'm tired and I need my sleep. Will you please go?'

'How about a lullaby, then?' Smiling softly, he leaned forward and she could smell the whiff of his expensive after-shave. Come on, Jo . . .'

'Damn it, Darren, do you want me to raise the house? I will, you know . . . !'

'What's going on here?'

They both turned towards the bathroom door to face Nicholas Hayward, still fully dressed.

'Nothing,' Jo snapped angrily. 'And you might knock next time you enter my room!'

'I did . . . you were too busy to hear me, apparently.'

'What do you want?'

'Peace and quiet. Your voice could raise the dead.' His eyes travelled insolently over her, sitting up in her T-shirt, and at Darren in his dressing-gown, his head only inches away from hers. 'You could lower your voices a fraction, you know. I know life can be great fun and all that, but I'd rather you kept it to yourself. Especially at night.'

'Oh, leave me alone!' Jo cried. 'Go away, and take him with you. I'm tired and—' and to her disgust she burst into tears of exhaustion.

The two men lapsed into silence. Nick was the first to speak. 'Come on, Darren, out you go. You're obviously not welcome here.' When she felt Darren's weight lifted off her bed she fell back against the pillows and buried her tears and her misery in their fresh whiteness.

'What's wrong with the kid?' Apparently this was a night for visitors. Andrea Burton was in her room as well.

'Nothing . . . she's had a rough day,' Nick said angrily. 'You're not needed here, Andrea.'

'Well, you were gone for such a long time, darling, I thought something was wrong,' the kittenish voice purred. 'You sure I can't help?'

'No!' Jo sat up and glared at the woman. 'Just let me go to sleep!'

'Of course, love. Come on, you men, out!' Andrea, sheathed in a gold satin dressing-gown, was pushing Darren out into the hall. 'I should have warned you about that, Jo darling. Never ever leave your door unlocked if you don't want nocturnal visitors. Come on, Nick, back to your room.'

In a minute they were both gone. The bathroom door was shut softly after them and no sounds came from behind it.

'So much for not "indulging" during filming,' Jo muttered disgustedly to herself. 'They make me sick . . . all of them!'

CHAPTER FIVE

AFTER two weeks in Elmfield Manor, Jo could only laugh at the faded memories of the first day's hardships and anxieties. She could hardly remember her worries or joys prior to the filming of Melissa. The film set had become her world, the crew and the cast her family. Everything else was reduced to a vaguely remembered dream.

The daily routine of make-up at dawn, filming all day, and the constant company of the crew in the evenings left her so exhausted that by the time she was allowed to crawl into bed she felt like an empty shell without past or future.

Even Emma had retreated into a sheltered corner of Jo's nagging conscience. Her letters, arriving regularly, were showing undeniable signs of good cheer and growing confidence, and though she still refused to talk of plans or activities, she seemed to know everything about Jo's progress and was warmly, genuinely delighted by it. Someone was certainly keeping her well informed, though Jo knew for certain that it couldn't have been Nick Hayward: ever since that first night at Elmfield, his manner had coldly denied any connections with her past or her family. When once, following Emma's instructions, Jo came to him with a letter she wanted delivered to her mother, he coldly asked her to give it to Ianikis' secretary. 'I'm not a post-box,' he said dryly, referring to her own churlish snipe at her audition.

As for her fears of further nocturnal encounters with him, he was as good as his word. He never 'indulged'—at least not with her. There were the usual speculations on set as to his ongoing affair with Andrea which the star did her best to confirm with veiled hints and excessive show of intimate affection outside the set, but Nick seemed to be keeping her at arm's length. Jo, who couldn't help keeping a very sensitive ear to the sounds in the director's bedroom, never noticed any suspicious sounds, but there was no guarantee that the two weren't meeting nightly in the star's room. Still, she was secretly delighted to note how sulky and bad-tempered Andrea had been prior to her departure at the end of the first week. Nick didn't even bother to see her off; he left the task to Ianikis.

Her admiration for Nick as a director grew daily. She rarely remembered now that he had ever played another role in her life. All she could think, if she had any energy or inclination to think at all after a day of hard labour, was how lucky she had been to have started her career under his guidance.

At first she kept feeling uneasy and disturbed when Nicholas would draw her aside to discuss her next scene, explain what he expected of her and listen to her own comments and ideas. These were the only moments she and he spent alone. But soon she learnt to ignore her instinctive reaction to his nearness and regard him only as her director.

He wasn't an indulgent one, either. If she didn't follow his demands quickly or intelligently enough, he would scold her impatiently in front of the whole crew, often reducing her to tears of rage. But there was nothing personal about it. They both knew that she was only an interpreter between him and his vision of Melissa.

From time to time, he would finish a certain shot and turn to her with something resembling his old intimate affection.

'That was good, Jo . . . we really got it this time.'

On these rare occasions, she would feel her new strength, her immunity to his disturbing masculinity gravely threatened, leaving her weak at the knees with foolish yearnings.

On the whole, she allowed little to interfere with her work on Melissa. Darren Williams remained a constant source of exasperation, but at least Andrea Burton was tucked away in Hollywood. And there was no further mention of those dreaded nude love scenes.

It was Sunday, and even in the topsy-turvy world of film-making the crew was expecting a slow, lazy day of rest after two harassing weeks. Yet no one raised any objection when the main hall gong sounded throughout the sleeping mansion, at six o'clock.

'What's going on?' Jo enquired sleepily, as her bed-side phone rang a few moments later.

'The sun, sweetie,' Lindsey informed her cheerfully. 'The sun has decided today of all days to honour us with a most glorious morning, and Nick was wondering whether you guys . . .'

'. . . wouldn't mind, etc., etc., etc.,' Jo completed the familiar opening. 'No, I don't mind. How about the others?'

'They don't mind either,' the assistant giggled. 'Apart from our dedication to the Art there's always the added bonus of extra pay on Sundays. And that's no laughing matter for hardworking beggars like us!'

'I know you,' Jo laughed. 'You'd do it for nothing. You're all masochists and so am I, and I love it! When do you want me down for make-up?'

'A minute ago, mate. So get into that blue muslin dress, and don't forget your drawers and your camisole. We're shooting the lake scene today.'

Jo hung up and groaned. This was one of the scenes she had been dreading: Melissa's seduction by Gilbert; Jo's first passionate love scene with Darren. The thought of Darren's touch made her shudder with loathing. For the life of her she couldn't imagine how she would bring herself to respond to his lovemaking. Well, she consoled herself, Melissa is an innocent child, really. She wouldn't be expected to show too much passion.

Lindsey was right. It was a glorious morning and the sun was making the best of the rain-drenched lawns and the luscious countryside that surrounded the small lake at the far end of the estate. It seemed a pity to spend such a rare spring morning making love to that detestable ego-maniac, Darren, instead of enjoying a well-earned rest. The colour of the lake reminded her of Nick's eyes, but she quickly swept the forbidden twinge under the carpet of her newly woven immunity.

Nick and Peter were whispering quietly by the camera, but stopped the moment they spotted her.

'Morning,' Nick's greeting was relaxed and friendly. 'Where's Darren?'

She bristled. 'How should I know?' Her ill-disguised loathing for the actor had become a joke among the crew, but Nicholas teasingly insisted on pretending that she and Darren had a thing going between them.

'He'll be here in a moment,' Lindsey answered. 'Still primping in front of the mirror, I guess.'

'I'm not,' Darren's sulky voice interrupted. 'I had to wait for her ladyship to finish with her make-up.' An insolent nod indicated Jo as the object of his complaint. 'She takes hours! I really don't see why I always have to be made up after her, Nick,' he tried appealing to the director. Darren was always surly in the mornings, but Jo knew that after a few shots he would start pestering her again with his ludicrously camp attentions.

'Stop moaning, Darren. I want to finish that darn lake scene today, so shape up,' Nick dismissed him.

'Yes, governor,' Darren grumbled. 'Anything you say.'

What came next threw both Jo and Darren into utter confusion. 'I want you to take a swim in the lake,' Nick announced calmly.

'You're mad!' Darren exploded after a stunned silence. 'My contract says nothing about freezing to death, Nick! The water must be icy, for God's sake!'

'Not you,' Nicholas discarded him. 'Only Jo . . . Do you think you could manage it?'

Just the idea of the cold, clear water made Jo's blood freeze in her veins. 'I . . , I guess so,' she said.

'Good girl,' he praised her. 'It'll make the scene far more effective—you in your camisole and drawers, your hair and body dripping wet, fished out of the water by Darren . . . I mean Gilbert. You'll be far more vulnerable to his assault and will save me the whole dreary business of trite preliminaries. We'll go for one shattering kiss and forget the usual mess of entwined limbs, exploring hands, and the rest of all that boring jazz.'

Silently, Jo thanked him. Nicholas's films were known for their delicate and sensitive handling of love-scenes, and yet she knew that today he had made this decision out of special consideration for her unspoken dread of explicit sex.

'We'll make sure you don't catch cold, Jo,' Nick was going on. 'Shall we try it?'

To her surprise she could hear the hesitation and uncertainty in his question. 'I can take it, Nick,' she reassured him. 'Honestly.'

'Here's what I'd like you to do, Jo . . .' He led her to a large willow tree which was only just beginning to dress up in beautifully fresh apple green leaves. 'Start by the shrub over there . . . walk towards the willow and stop. You know you're early for your rendezvous with Gilbert . . . and the water looks very inviting, so let me see the idea taking shape in your mind, then take off your dress and your shoes and stockings and step down into the water.' He turned to Peter. 'I want it all in one long shot, Peter, so make sure you have plenty of film in that contraption of yours.'

'Got it,' said Peter.

'And Jo, take all the time in the world, will you? I want it slow . . . very slow and natural.'

'All right,' Jo echoed.

They rehearsed the scene several times, just for moves and for camera positions, and then, as usual, she had to wait until the crew and Peter were ready. Finally, Peter gave his usual peddler holler: 'Ready when you are, boss!'

'Action!' Nick called.

Coolly, aware of her pace and timing, Jo made her way from the shrub to the willow, shed her dress, then sat down, spreading her legs like a guileless child, to take off her slippers and white silk stockings. She had learnt to move like an awkward adolescent, remembering her own clumsiness at the age of fifteen. Then in her long drawers and lacy comisole, she walked gingerly over the rough ground, flinched when she stepped on a sharp stone and stopped to rub her sore foot. She could hear Nick's murmur of approval behind her. They were not using sound for that shot.

Straightening up, she reached the edge of the lake and gasped as her bare foot encountered the icy water.

'Don't try to hide it, Jo,' Nick called out. 'Cold water is cold water even in Regency England, you know. Melissa can feel the cold just like you.'

Clenching her teeth, her eyes shut tight, Jo lowered herself into the deep lake. Every grimace, every twinge was faithfully recorded by the camera, just as Nicholas intended it to.

When she got used to the icy temperature, she turned herself on her back and began floating towards the centre of the lake. Forgetting herself for a moment, she raised her head and threw Nick a delighted smile. She could see him nodding at her in approval.

'Cut!' his voice came a few seconds later. 'Now, stay there, Jo . . . only for a few more seconds.'

Those few seconds seemed like an eternity. She was beginning to worry that she would catch a cramp if she remained much longer in the water.

'Right, Jo,' at last Nick shouted at her. 'Swim back towards us, and smile . . . as you did before. You're supposed to have spotted Gilbert waiting for you on the bank. When you get here, reach for Darren's hand and he'll pull you out. Got that?'

'Yes,' she called back, her teeth clicking noisily. 'Only hurry up—I'm beginning to freeze!'

'Action!' His shout was harsh with concern.

Fighting the current and the numbness in her limbs, she swam towards the bank, smiled at Darren, her lips stiff with cold, and allowed him to drag her out.

'Cut. That was great, honey!'

As if released by an electric switch, her body reacted with a violent attack of shivers. She had never been so cold in her life.

A large wool blanket was thrown over her shaking body and over her dripping head, and suddenly she was swept by strong arms to rest against Nick's hard, throbbing chest. For a second he just kept her held tightly against the warmth of his own body, and then his arms began rubbing her vigorously, forcing the blood to resume its normal circulation. In a daze, she let herself lean closer, ready to melt into his pulsating, vibrantly alive flesh. She buried her face in his soft cashmere sweater, willing his thumping heart to calm her own shudders. It was all she wanted. Just the nearness of Nick, the warmth that flowed from him and the feel of his hands as they rubbed life into her back, her arms, her thighs.

Gradually, as the violent shudders began to subside, she became aware of a new sensation which made her skin and blood tingle not only with new life but with a long-forgotten thrill.

A shameful shudder of thrill replaced the earlier sense of safety as she suddenly identified her sensual response to Nick's touch. Writhing to get away from his embrace, she averted her face to hide the naked need that showed in her eyes.

'That was a veritable baptism,' he whispered down at her, his voice husky and unsteady. 'I shouldn't have made you do it, honey.'

'Oh, I'm fine,' she found strength in his harsh concern. 'I'll be all right in a second.' Raising her eyes, she encountered his blue gaze, anxious, full of self-blame, and she smiled, indicating that she could manage now on her own.

'Here, Nick, let me take care of her,' Lindsey was beside her, and she was no longer shielded by the radiating warmth of his body. Instead, she was led to her folding chair, wrapped in a new, dry blanket; a mug of steaming coffee was thrust into her hand.

'I don't think we should go on,' Nick was saying quietly. 'I can't let her go through the day soaked to the skin. I'll think of another way of shooting the scene. Take her back to the house, Lindsey . . .'

'No!' In one sweeping gesture, Jo threw the blanket away and stood up. 'I'm fine, Nick. Really.' And to her own amazement, she realised that she was . . . full of revived energy and vibrating with a secret, undefined spark of incredible joy.

'I don't think so,' he grumbled.

'Well, I am. I'm not the first actress to go into a freezing cold lake. Just don't ask me to do it again!'

The look in his troubled eyes sent a wave of melting liquid down the pit of her stomach. 'Sure?'

She nodded. And suddenly his intent eyes crinkled into that old, lazy smile which hardly touched his chiselled lips. 'Then let's do it, damn it. Lindsey!' His voice rose to its usual commanding drawl. 'Get buckets of hot water and keep it hot. We'll keep her clothes and hair damp and turn on all the sunlamps we have to keep her reasonably warm. Where the hell is Darren!'

'Here,' Darren stepped forward.

The next hour passed in filming insignificant shots,

just inserts which would link her coming out of the lake, dripping water, with the main section of the scene. After each take, Lindsey kept drenching her with a bucketful of wonderfully warm water, to retain the illusion of time.

'Right,' Nick announced at last, 'let's tackle the main course now.'

Jo had as yet no inkling of the nightmare which awaited her. It started just like any other shot, with Nick giving her and Darren dry technical instructions.

'Start by holding her at arm's length, Darren. Look into her eyes for as long as you can hold it, then slide the straps of her camisole off her shoulders, and slowly draw her to you; take her face in your hands and—in your own time—have your kiss.' He now turned to Jo. 'You just let Darren guide you, honey. He'll know what to do. Just respond to him, that's all.'

'Nick,' Darren intervened.

'What is it?'

'What . . . what kind of a kiss?'

Nick stared at him, his lips curling in exasperated contempt. 'Oh, you can give it your all this time. Lucky fellow, aren't you?' His voice was lazy and cool as usual, but it held a tinge of cold anger.

And then the nightmare began. For the first time since they had started shooting, Jo felt utterly debilitated. She just couldn't let herself go. Melissa simply refused to materialise, to be aroused by her passionate seducer. It was Jo, still tingling with the memory of Nick's body against hers, who stubbornly remained in the foreground, detesting Darren's smooth hands and recoiling from the touch of his lips on hers. She couldn't blame Darren this time. The actor was totally professional, unflaggingly patient. Yet she couldn't bring herself to respond.

'This is hopeless!' Nick shouted after the sixth take. 'What the hell is the matter with you, Jo? Can't you co-operate a little?'

'I'm . . . I'm sorry,' she stammered, 'I just can't manage it.'

'What do you mean, can't manage it?' He was towering over her, actually shouting at her, something he had never done before. 'Just let the man kiss you and respond. What's so bloody difficult about that?'

They tried once more, but it was hopeless. Again Nick stopped them sharply as Jo, by now rigid with the dreaded anticipation of the coming embrace, wouldn't even let Darren draw her to him.

'You bitch!' Darren hissed, thoroughly disgusted with her, as Nick shouted 'Cut' again.

Nick was clutching his fair, thick hair, as if about to tear it off in frustration. 'Sorry,' she said. 'It's no use—I can't do it.'

A long, dead silence followed her mutinous declaration.

'Oh, can't you?' Nick spoke at last, his voice low and tight. 'God, Jo, you had no such problems at the age of sixteen, if I remember rightly!'

It took a second before it dawned on her that he was referring to that horrible night in Corfu.

'I hate you, Nick!'

An unfamiliar strangled voice rang through the silence. It was hers.

The one thing she didn't expect was to see his furious expression replaced by a sudden, amused smile. He had been standing by the camera but now reached her side in two long, purposeful strides and looked down at her, dangerously quiet. 'I think I know what to do,' he said, not to her but to himself. She turned her eyes away, to hide her fear.

'Look at me,' he was caressing her with that old Nick's voice. 'Look into my eyes, Jo.'

As if hypnotised, she lifted her head.

With a deft but gentle gesture he pushed the damp hair which tumbled over on her forehead, then his hands came down on her shoulders and slowly slid the wet straps of her camisole, allowing his hands to roam down her upper arms to hold them in a firm, warm grip.

For an endless moment she stood imprisoned by his gaze, aware of nothing but its depth. She was no longer afraid. The crew, Darren, the camera had all retired behind a screen of thick mist. There was only his cool, teasing smile, his blue eyes and the burning touch of his hands on her arms.

But, in a flash, the teasing smile was gone, leaving his face raw and naked. She saw his eyes widening, darkening in a sudden shock of instant hungry urge, turning black with intensity as they slid down, leaving her unblinking stare, to devour her mouth.

Her heart stopped beating. Her lips parted in response to an unspoken command. His face became a hazy blur as it drew nearer, and then her face was gripped by two hands and she shut her eyes, in a dazed anticipation of their long-awaited reunion.

Softly, carefully, Nick let his lips rest on hers, barely kissing, the tip of his tongue lightly tracing their shape, urging, teasing, until her arms came up to bury their fingers in his thick, warm hair and her lips came to meet

GET
4 BOOKS
FREE

LOVE BEYOND REASON
There was a surprise in store for Amy!

Amy had thought nothing could be as perfect as the days she had shared with Vic Hoyt in New York City—before he took off for his Peace Corps assignment in Kenya.

Impulsively, Amy decided to follow. She was shocked to find Vic established in his new life. . . and interested in a new girl friend.

Amy faced a choice: be smart and go home. . . or stay and fight for the only man she would ever love.

MAN OF POWER
Sara took her role seriously

Although Sara had already planned her esc from the subservient posi in which her father's death had placed her, Morgan Haldane's timely appear had definitely made it ea

All Morgan had asked in return was that she pose a fiancée. He'd confessed t needing protection from partner's wife, Louise, and part of Sara's job proved e

But unfortunately for heart, Morgan ha told her about Monique. . .

Your Romantic Adventure Starts Here.

THE LEO MAN
"He's every bit as sexy as his father!"

Her grandmother thought that description would appeal to Rowan, but Rowan was determined to avoid any friendship with the arrogant James Fraser.

Aboard his luxury yacht, that wasn't easy. When they were all shipwrecked on a tropical island, it proved impossible.

And besides, if it weren't for James, none of them would be alive. Rowan was confused. Was it merely gratitude that she now felt for this strong and rugged man?

THE WINDS O WINTER
She'd had so much— now she had no

Anne didn't dwell on it, b the pain was still with her—double-edged pain of gr and rejection.

It had greatly altered her, Anne barely resembled t girl who four years earlier left her husband, David. probably wouldn't even recognize her—especially with another name.

Anne made up her mind just *had* to go to his house discover if what she suspe was true. . .

These FOUR free Harlequin Romance novels allow you to enter the world of romance, love and desire. As a member of the Harlequin Home Subscription Plan, you can continue to experience all the moods of love. You'll be inspired by moments so real... so moving... you won't want them to end. So start your own Harlequin Romance adventure by returning the reply card below. <u>DO IT TODAY!</u>

his, her whole body throbbing again with overwhelming, vividly-remembered moist sweetness.

Three long years seemed to have evaporated as she once again began to drown in the incredible enchantment of their mutual hunger. Once again she moaned with shocked delight as they strove to penetrate into the innermost depth of their separate beings. She was slowly sinking into a dark, whirling well of joy, held only by the vicelike hands.

'Hey, governor, isn't that supposed to be my scene?' Darren's tight chuckle seemed to come from a great distance, through a thick mist of whirling senses. 'Shall I take over now?'

Suddenly Jo was alone, exposed, naked. Slowly she opened her eyes and saw the smiling faces of the crew, caught a few stifled giggles and finally encountered Peter's sympathetic grin. He seemed to be the only one to realise how deeply she had been affected. Nick himself was back in his place by the camera, his face blank, expressionless, his eyes opaque.

'I think you won't have any problems now,' he said calmly to Darren.

It meant nothing to him. That hungry, devouring kiss, that union after so many years of separation, had nothing to do with Nicholas Hayward. He was only interested in tantalising, arousing his actress so as to pass her, vibrating with sensual yearnings, to his leading actor. The pain that welled inside her was excruciating, yet she could do nothing; even the tears refused to flow.

'Shall we try it again?' she heard him enquire politely.

It took a long moment before she could find her voice. 'I think so.' She took a deep breath and deftly repeated her confirmation: 'Yes, I'm sure I'll manage it now.'

'Good girl,' Nick smiled tightly. His gaze tried to transmit a message, responding to the look of utter despondency in her large eyes. Sincere regret came out in a hard, strangled voice. 'Oh, let's get on with it, then. I want this damned nuisance over and done with before lunch break.'

The spell broke. Everyone started moving about. Jo was left alone, with Darren at her side.

'You certainly have it in you when you put your mind to it, don't you?' Darren gritted through his teeth, his smile ugly with fury.

'It must have been the cold water, Darren,' she answered him, almost calm now. 'You try and show passion when you're shivering with cold! It'll be all right now, I promise.'

'It'd better be,' he whispered. 'I refuse to do another take. If this one is no good, Nick can look for another Gilbert. I've had it!'

'He'll probably prefer to look for another Melissa,' she answered. 'So don't worry.'

'Are you ready there?' Nicholas was calling.

'Yes, Nick,' she called back.

'Right then, take number nine.' He raised his arm, like an orchestra conductor. 'Once more, then. And this time, Jo . . . with feeling!'

Back at last in the privacy of her hotel room, Jo sank on the bed and lay there, her eyes staring wide open at the ornate ceiling. I love him, the thought kept drumming dully through her aching head. It's no use denying it or fighting it any more. She loved Nicholas Hayward, the man who had once been as close to her as a father, the man who had so ruthlessly betrayed her mother . . . her director. She had loved him for years, even as a gawky teenager, but now her feelings were far deeper, far more desperate, and excruciatingly painful.

Tears began to flow silently at the slowly dawning premonition of the months, the years ahead of her, with that unrelenting devouring pain of hopeless longings. No amount of hard work, no fame or success could relieve that torment. This kind of love, she knew, the love of an adult to her childhood hero, was not something one could get over easily.

Her only hope now was for Nick to maintain his impersonal indifference towards her. He wasn't likely to ask her to work for him again, and as long as he didn't develop a sudden attack of revived affection for what she had once been, she at least would be spared the torture of his presence.

The last thing she wanted that evening was to join Peter and Lindsey on a night out in Stratford. She had promised to go with them but tried to cry off, desperately in need to be left alone after the shattering events of the morning.

'I think you should come, Jo,' Peter insisted quietly. 'I know how you feel, but—'

'What do you mean?'

He smiled an awkward attempt to comfort her. 'Come on, Jo. This is only a passing infatuation. You'll forget all about him the moment you start your next film. You're not the only girl to fall in love with the director of her first film.'

So Peter thought she was just an inexperienced actress, infatuated with her first director and simply shaken by the calculating ruthlessness of his technique.

'He had to get you over that aversion to Darren some-how. We would still have been working on that scene otherwise.' He shook her gently. 'Come on, love. You shouldn't be left alone tonight.'

'All right,' she capitulated, 'I'll be down in ten minutes.'

Stratford's most illustrious son was still drawing throngs of theatre-lovers and tourists to his lovely home-town. And the Swan restaurant was swarming with the usual crowd of Royal Shakespeare Company members and fans who wanted to be near their idols. It was a natural favourite place for the film crew on their rare forays into civilisation.

'Oh, no!' Jo groaned as the first face she saw was that of Darren. He was sitting alone at the bar, sulkily nursing a whisky tumbler.

'We'd better get out before he sees us,' Lindsey suggested.

They were too late. A large party of the film crew, seated around a long table, had spotted them, and there was no escaping their loud, welcoming shrieks.

'Hey, Jo, Peter, Lindsey! Come and join us!'

'Sorry, Jo. We're in for it,' Peter whispered as he led her towards the table. She turned to him, a little per-plexed by his anxious apology. 'He's here too.'

She was grateful to him for warning her. By the time she met Nick's deep blue eyes, she had already braced herself. He was sitting between the chief gaffer and Francis Blakely so that she wasn't forced to sit next to him, but she was painfully aware of his presence across the table. It was hard to keep her eyes from straying in his direction.

'Are you all right, Jo?' Nick turned on her, impersonal and coolly polite. 'No after-effects?' She stared at him woodenly. 'I mean, no cold or sneezes or heavy limbs?'

'Oh,' she breathed. For a moment she thought he was referring to his kiss. 'No, no . . . I've forgotten all about it.'

'I bet you wouldn't like a repeat performance, though,' Francis chuckled. 'Nick says you were blue . . . literally blue, when they fished you out.'

'It won't show in the film, will it?' she asked Nicholas, adopting a detached, professional tone.

'No. On the whole, I think it's going to be one of your best scenes.' He smiled at her, but his smile was tight and cold. He hurriedly looked away as if the memory of the morning had left a bad taste in his mouth.

The waiter created a diversion. And soon Jo found that by keeping her attention on Peter and his conversation, she could keep the back of her head as a fence between her and Nick.

They were drinking their coffee when she realised that Peter had stopped talking and was watching her silently. 'Sorry,' she shook herself, 'I'm afraid I haven't been listening, Peter.'

'You're crying into your coffee, you idiot,' he told her. 'What am I going to do with you?' His arm gently encircled her shoulders. 'You'll get over him, love. Give it a day or two. We all fall in and out of love faster than we change our jeans. That's the name of the game in film-making. I'm not having such a good time myself, you know.' She lifted her eyes and caught him unawares, the naked look of yearning was unmistakable.

'Oh, God, Peter—I'm sorry.' If it weren't so terribly painful, she would have laughed. They all seemed to be performing in a Shakespearean comedy: Peter in love with her, Lindsay in love with Peter, she herself hopelessly in love with Nick.

Peter misinterpreted her stricken expression. 'Don't worry about me, love. I'll cope . . . and maybe one day, who knows . . .'

She leaned forward and gave him a light kiss on the cheek. He seemed the only friend she had in the world right now. They were two lost souls in the labyrinth of misery and hopeless love. His arm tightened around her shoulder.

'Well, well, well, I seem to have dropped in at the right moment!' The empty chair next to hers was dragged noisily and Darren, holding a tall whisky tumbler, settled heavily on it, grinning at her. 'How about letting me in on the fun, sweetheart? You're obviously in the right mood today, for a change!'

'Leave her alone, Darren,' Peter snapped at him, his smile freezing in anger.

'Why should I? I worked hard enough on her to be entitled to a slice of the cake myself. Come on, darling, let's have one too, or would you prefer to do it outside, in my car?'

A second later he was nursing his jaw, his mouth gaping in pained amazement. Peter was on his feet, his first still clenched. 'Leave her alone, you second-class Casanova . . . just get out of here!'

By the look on Darren's face, Jo knew there was going to be a fist-fight in a moment. She jumped to her feet, trying to position herself in Peter's way, and at the same moment saw Nick get up.

She wasn't very clear as to the rest of the fight. But suddenly Darren's body was sprawling on the ground,

Peter was being dragged out by Lindsey and she herself was encircled in Nick's arms.

'Come on, Jo. I'd better take you home.'

She had never been inside the white Porsche before, though it had become a very familiar landmark at the hotel parking lot. She had come to look for it every night before going to bed, to reassure herself that Nick was in the hotel, just a bathroom away from her.

She settled next to him, keeping her eyes glued to the window. He hadn't said a word yet and by the look of it she suspected he would say even less during the long drive to Elmfield.

She was wrong. As they left Stratford's busy streets behind them, he broke the silence. 'Lay off Peter, Jo.'

'*What?*' She was prepared for mockery, impersonal small-talk, but certainly not for that.

'I can't believe you've changed so much as to enjoy tormenting a perfectly defenceless victim.'

'But I'm not . . . I'm not!' she choked.

'You're leading him on . . . Or else—' he slowed down, and turned to look at her, 'or else you feel the same way about him.'

'I like him . . . he's been my only friend here, while you . . . you—'

He wasn't interested. 'How about that little exhibition at the table tonight? Was that your way of showing him that you're just a "friend"?'

It can't be real, she said to herself. Here I am, tearing my heart out because of a hopeless, foolish love for this cold man, and he's accusing me of toying with his cameraman. He's actually protecting Peter from me!

'Oh, God!' she exploded finally, her throat tight. 'I'm

glad I've found out all about filming so early. Because—'
she started to stumble over her own sobs, 'because I
never want to make another film again. Never! One has
to be a robot, a heartless, numb robot to take this kind of
torture!'

Silently, Nick swerved off the road and turned the
ignition off. 'Torture?' he asked, mildly astonished.
'Aren't you enjoying it?'

'I hate it!'

He thought for a moment. 'Your mother isn't a senseless, heartless robot, is she? And yet she's been working
in films for years.'

'Don't you dare mention my mother!' she was screaming now. 'At least have the decency to shut up about
her!'

'Sorry,' he said seriously. 'We'll confine our chat only
to you. So you don't want to make any more films . . .'
he paused, weighing the idea in his mind. 'I can't say that
makes me very unhappy, you know.'

'Why?' She sat up.

'Well, if I had my way, you wouldn't have become an
actress at all. I don't want you obsessed by the profession
like your mo—sorry, sorry,' he hurriedly apologised,
raising his hands in mock surrender.

'Why not?' she bristled.

'I'd rather answer that when we finish this damn film.'
Suddenly his anger was back between them. He was no
longer in cool control of the situation. 'I'm sick and tired
of the whole bloody thing. I wish I never started it . . .
and I could kick myself for being foolish enough to put
you in it!'

'But why?' Jo was aroused, momentarily, from her
misery, her hopeless love for him. 'I thought you liked

me. You said I was good . . . why, only today you told me that—'

'Oh, damn you!'

There was nothing sweet and patient about his kiss, nothing of the heady exploration of the morning. Her lips were being crushed painfully against her teeth, and the pain made her gasp. He didn't seem to hear her; he assulted her mouth while his hands, angry and cruelly hungry, pushed her away from him so that he could cup her breasts. No man had ever touched her before, and his grasp was too raw, too naked to arouse any pleasure. Unprepared for the sharp pain, she groaned.

She was immediately released.

'Now you see why,' he rasped. His voice was unsteady, and he was struggling to regain control over himself. Even his hands, as he replaced them on the steering, seemed to shake. 'Don't you ever provoke me again, Jo Montague! Next time I won't let you off so easily.'

'I wouldn't want you to,' she whispered, forgetting her pain for a moment in an elated thrill of triumph.

'Wouldn't you? You want to emerge out of your first film as the director's latest bedmate? Do you have any idea how badly this will affect your career?'

'I don't care . . . I just want you to . . . to want me,' she managed to say, amazed by her own audacity. 'You do want me, don't you?'

'Yes, I want you . . . and so does Peter and so does Darren and so would dozens of other men on every film you'll be shooting.' Calm again, Nick switched the car on and they were back on the road. 'Take a page from my book, honey. Keep us all at arm's length during working hours. Sex isn't good for business.'

Like a balloon pricked by a pin, Jo felt her elation ooze out, leaving her flat and confused. She moved away from him as far as she could, letting the cold hardness of the Porsche window cool her burning cheeks.

She was hardly aware they had reached Elmfield. His hand pulling her out of the car shook her out of her numb misery.

'One more thing, Jo,' he said quietly as he half led, half pushed her towards the house. 'I'm sorry about this morning. I didn't mean to be so thorough with you.'

'That's all right,' she mumbled.

'I just want you to know that it hit me as hard as it hit you. I've never lost control over myself on set before. So don't feel too badly about it, Jo, I wasn't just toying with you.'

It was cold comfort. Knowing that he wanted her only made her love for him even more desperate. She was just another young and desirable infatuated actress he would have gladly taken to his bed, but couldn't be bothered. Not while he was busy making a film.

CHAPTER SIX

'MOVIES make money because they sell illusions,' Nick had said once, years ago. 'The greatest illusion, though, is not the product, but the world of film-making itself. We start all starry-eyed, eager to become one of the great happy family on set, and end up exhausted and flat. And yet we're always impatient to rush into the next film, deluding ourselves that this one will be different.'

Jo had ample opportunity to confirm the truth of his statement. Her initial enchantment with film-making was sorely tested after that disastrous evening in Stratford. She was still obsessed with the character of Melissa and just as eager to give her all in front of the cameras. But somehow she had lost the pleasure of being a member of the film-crew family.

She now only came alive on set, thriving on the excruciating hours spent in Nick's presence, tormented by his indifference, yet hopelessly trapped by her admiration and love for him. At times she wished this exquisite torture could be over and she could be free to crawl back home and lick her wounds away from this bustling, busy world. But the thought a life away from him, bereft of those hours spent together, even if her presence was only acknowledged by that coolly critical glance of the artist inspecting his inanimate creation, would throw her into utter despair.

Andrea Burton returned to Elmfield Manor before she had been expected, and he buted a lot to Jo's general sense of discontent and isolation. Andrea made it quite clear that Nicholas Hayward had insisted on it. 'He had asked Eric to write two extra scenes for me . . .' she confided sweetly, making sure Jo could hear her. 'One love scene with Darren and a good violent quarrel with you, Francis.'

'I thought you were busy shooting in Hollywood till the end of the month,' Francis Blakely remarked dryly. He had never tried to disguise his hostility towards the star.

'I was, darling, but I managed to squirm out of it. You know how it is with Nick . . . when he calls, you simply have to come.'

Ironically, the more tormented Jo felt, the better she was at her work. Every evening, as she watched the developed 'rushes' of the previous day's shooting, she was aware of her own growing strength as an actress. Melissa was developing daily into a well-defined, sensitively portrayed character. She had become real . . . far more real than Jo Montague, at least as far as Nick Hayward was concerned. He had even begun addressing her on set as Melissa, remembering her real-life name only to criticise her. And these occasions were becoming far too frequent.

P . . . he was not the only one to feel the scourge of the d . . . . . . rowing exasperation with the whole production . . . . . . been driving his actors harder than ever, ... m one scene to another, as if he was . . . . . . e devil. Under the usual cool, lazy . . . . . . ng more and more relentless, ... patient.

. . . . . . eet from six in the morn-
. . . . . . ing to show signs of

exhaustion. Yet the more they resented him, the better they worked, determined to show him that they could match his unflagging energy.

Besides, under the disguise of moanings and bad-mouthing, they all nurtured the deepest admiration and loyalty for their general.

'What the hell is the matter with the man?' Francis Blakely grumbled to Jo, as once more they were asked to work late into the night. 'He's rushing through the script like a maniac!'

'He's probably in a hurry to get it over and done with so that he can take Jo away from here,' suggested Darren, too tired to smooth his heavy sarcasm with one of his old charmer's smiles. 'Hayward never indulges during shooting, or haven't you heard?'

Andrea threw Jo a brittle, angry smile. 'There are rumours to the contrary, darling.'

'Can't you lay off, both of you?' Francis snapped at them. 'Leave the girl alone!'

'Oh, get lost!' Darren stalked away. He had stopped pestering Jo, with his amorous advances after that evening at the Swan, but still kept worrying her with his cynical, coarse insinuations, generally connected with Nicholas. Once or twice she caught him and Andrea whispering together, staring at her with hostility which she found disturbingly menacing.

'Next time I sign for a film,' Jo commented dryly, 'I'll put in one condition: no Darren Williams. Thank God he's stopped pestering me, but his temper is absolutely foul!'

'Oh, he's a little put out by Nick cutting him out of three scenes. Apparently he won't be coming back after the weekend.'

Jo stared at him. 'I didn't know about it. Why?'

'Well, the official reason is that Darren has other commitments and Nick's agreed to let him go. My guess is that Nick's simply got tired of his endless moaning. So that's at least one ray of sunlight in this ghastly mess . . . Darren won't be around to annoy you any more.' Francis looked at the tired girl with a wry smile. 'Aren't you overjoyed?'

'I'm too tired to smile.' Jo groaned, rubbing her aching shoulders. 'We haven't done our wedding scene yet. By the time we get to it, I'll probably fall asleep in your arms out of sheer exhaustion!'

'Oh,' Francis looked at her. 'We aren't going to do the wedding scene. It's been cut—didn't you know?'

Nothing is more distressing to an actress than to lose a single line. To have a whole scene cut out was downright degrading.

'Lindsey,' Jo turned to the director-assistant, who was devouring an improvised evening snack with the appetite of a starved farmhorse, 'is it true?'

'Oh, yes,' Lindsey didn't stop munching vigorously, 'didn't I tell you? He's decided today . . . and incidentally, I was also asked to tell you that you can go home for the weekend. Nick won't be needing you till Tuesday.'

Disappointment cut through Jo like a sharp knife. 'He . . . he doesn't need me?'

'No, Nick's going to work with Andrea . . . she's got two scenes added. So you're off the hook for a few days.'

Jo registered only the first news. 'You mean, he's cancelled one of my scenes and has given Andrea two extra?'

Jo's distress broke through the assistant's absentmindedness. 'Oh, Jo, I'm sorry. But you mustn't take it badly—it happens all the time.'

Jo remained silent for a second, then turned on Lindsey intently. 'What's the real reason, Lindsey? Why am I being squeezed out?'

'You're not being . . .' Lindsey started to protest, but then, seeing Jo's expression, gave up. 'I don't know, Joey. Perhaps it's because you require more work than the more experienced actors, or perhaps—'

'Yes?' Jo prompted her.

'Forget it, sweetie. I'd better not interfere.'

'Is it my acting? Isn't he pleased with the results?'

Lindsey's patience snapped. One of her most tiresome functions as assistant director was to reassure the huge, anxious ego of the stars. 'Don't you start, Jo! I have enough on my hands having to mollycoddle Darren and Andrea, without you asking for a dose of ego-boosting. You're good . . . you're excellent, to be quite precise. And you know it. So please—'

They were shooting indoors that day, in one of the smaller rooms which had been set up as Sir John Casenove's master bedroom. Nicholas was trying to finish all the scenes which were taking place on this specific set to avoid a further waste of time in resetting it at a later stage. Andrea and Francis, in the roles of Sir John and his promiscuous wife, Helena, carried the bulk of the work.

The bedroom was overcrowded, bursting at the seams with heavy lighting and camera equipment and an army of technicians, grips and gaffers. There was hardly a square foot of superfluous space and Jo knew her presence there was only an unnecessary impediment. The rules of the game specified that she remained put unless

Nick Hayward said he wouldn't be needing her any more. But when one of the junior electricians politely asked her for the second time to kindly not get under his feet, she gave up.

The moment her body hit her bed, she fell asleep. She had learnt to grab every idle moment to make up for short nights and excruciatingly long days.

'Wake up, Jo!' Lindsey shook her impatiently out of her sleep. 'They're all waiting for you.'

Jo allowed herself to be dragged downstairs again. 'What's happening now?' She could no longer follow Nick's hectic, seemingly irrational filming sequences.

'Your scene with Francis—the bedroom scene. What the hell made you disappear like that, Jo? You know we were doing it tonight.'

'Well, I didn't think you'd be finished with Andrea . . .'

'Don't think, sweetie. You should have learnt that much by now. Nick's been screaming for you for at least five minutes.'

'No!' Jo gasped in mock-horror. 'As long as that? I'll never be able to face the world again!' Lindsey wasn't amused.

Nick hardly looked at her when she hurried on to the set. 'So there you are,' he said dryly, too disgusted to reward her with a few angry words. 'Let's not waste any more time. You might be brimming with pent-up energy, but these people here have been working hard all day, so don't keep them waiting any longer.'

She refused to apologise. 'Get into your shift,' he ordered shortly. 'And leave your face as it is. Your hair too. I want it long and lose.'

The dresser was waiting for her, looking upset and

disgruntled. Nicholas had plainly given them all hell for having let her disappear like that. 'I'm sorry, Dora,' Jo tried to cajole the woman into her usual good humour. 'How was I to know that he'd decide to use me again? It's almost nine o'clock!'

'You're telling me! I've been on my feet since six, and I'm getting sick and tired of the whole thing. Go on, girl, get into your shift. This is the last shot for today, thank God. If the governor doesn't change his mind again, that is.'

Jo was about to pull the flowing, thin white nightgown over her brief pants and bra, when a familiar voice purred from behind her: 'I'd get rid of the bra, love. I don't think it would look right in an early nineteenth-century setting.'

Popping her head out of the shift, Jo stared at Andrea. 'No one will see it, under the shift,' she argued, seething inwardly at the star's freshness and stunning looks even after twelve hours of hard labour.

'That's where you're wrong, darling. You won't be wearing this shift for long.'

Jo stifled a gasp as the first bud of panic began hammering in her mind. 'What do you mean?'

'You're supposed to take it off, aren't you?' The beautiful face was smiling at her innocently.

'I didn't know about that,' Dora broke in. 'Nobody tells me anything. Well, come on, Jo, don't just gape at me. Take that bra off—'

Since the first day, when Darren had teased her about an ominous nude love scene, Jo had been living in dread of it. But as no one had ever mentioned it again, she began to relax. Finally she convinced herself that the whole thing was nothing but a poor joke.

'There's nothing in the script about stripping in this scene,' she protested huskily.

'You tell Nick that, my love,' Andrea answered coolly, carefully taking off her costume. 'Why don't you take a good stiff drink? I always do . . . One drink of whisky and I don't give a damn any more. Have you got some, Dora?' she asked the dresser, as she covered her half-naked body in the familiar gold satin dressing-gown.

Numbly, Jo let the dresser put a paper cup in her hand and watched her fill it to the brim. 'Go on, love, take a good sip. By the time you're finished that, you won't care if they have you swinging naked from the chandelier!'

The unfamiliar choking liquid burnt her insides as it slowly seeped down into her stomach, leaving her slightly dazed, her ears ringing faintly.

'Go on, Jo, drink it up,' Andrea urged her.

Jo took another sip. This time she didn't choke, though the taste was just as foul. She gulped half the cup and breathed in relief as the ringing in her ears began to subside.

'Are you ready, Jo?' Lindsey was suddenly in the room, looking a little blurred.

'I'm ready,' Jo articulated carefully.

'Your bra,' Andrea reminded her.

'Oh, yes, my bra,' she smiled. And sliding her arms out of the full sleeves, she slipped off her bra under the tent-like cover of the shift. 'Let's go,' she stated solemnly, pushing her arms back into the sleeves.

'Come on, then.'

As she stepped past the full mirror, she caught sight of herself. The shift covered her completely, from chin to bare feet; but with the harsh light behind her, the flimsy muslin did nothing to hide the curves of her hips, the rounded mounds of her small breasts . . . and the darker shade of her nipples. 'Take another sip,' Andrea advised, helping to raise the paper cup to Jo's lips. From above the rim, she hazily noted Lindsey's amazed look.

'You never drink, Jo,' she reminded her.

'That's right—I don't.'

'Well, don't get too sloshed,' Lindsey said dryly. 'I don't think Nick would appreciate it. He's in no mood for any more trouble tonight.'

Nick's name filled her with defiant determination. 'I'll be fine . . . let's go.'

Not too steady on her feet, she clung on to Lindsey, using the girl's slight body as a shield. She kept the paper cup gripped tightly in her hand.

For once she had the gratification of seeing everyone jump up the moment she walked in. They had plainly been sitting idly, waiting for her to arrive.

Francis, looking splendid in black breeches, highly polished Hessian boots and wide-sleeved shirt, was lounging on top of the large bed, smoking a thin cigar. Jo gave him a bright, happy smile.

'Sir John, I presume,' she cried from the other end of the room, in a false upper-class simper. 'So sorry to have kept you waiting.'

Her bright greeting drew some amazed looks from the crew. Nick, from his usual stand by the camera, looked at her thoughtfully. 'Have you been drinking?' he asked.

Lindsey answered for her. 'I'm afraid so, Nick.'

'Good God, Jo!' For a moment she struggled with his strong hand as it tried to prise the cup from her clenched hand. 'Have you gone completely mad?'

'No,' she explained. 'At least, I don't think I have.'

He turned away from her, giving the empty paper cup to Lindsey. 'This girl is going to drive me out of my mind one of these days,' he remarked calmly. 'Do you think you can understand me, Jo?'

'Oh, yes, I can understand you, Nicky.' She smiled at him, trustingly.

He groaned, shaking his head in disbelief. 'I'm sorry about this, guys,' he announced to the world at large. 'I'm not sure I can handle her.'

Jo rearranged her face to look attentive and serious. 'Look, Nick, I'm fine, see? Now, what do you want me to do?'

He sighed tiredly. 'Just get on that bed, beside Francis, and kneel on it . . .' Reeling slightly, she obeyed him. The soft bed gave in under her weight and she almost fell on top of Francis. She started to giggle.

'Stop it, Jo! For God's sake, will you behave yourself?' In spite of his impatience, she detected a note of amused affection in his voice. Warmed up by it, she turned to him and gave him a loving smile. 'Don't crouch on your haunches, dear. You're not a frog about to turn into a prince . . .'

'It's the other way round,' she corrected him.

She still refused to sit up, as he wanted. The most she agreed to do was to raise her shoulders slightly, but she stubbornly kept her arms clenched tightly around her chest, determined to shield her breasts, covered only by the thin transparent shift, from the glaring spotlights.

'I said sit up, damn you! Can't you understand plain English? And stop hugging yourself in that ridiculous manner!'

Suddenly he was beside her, forcibly pulling her by the

shoulders to an upright position, and pulling her arms away from her body.

'No,' she cried out, 'don't!'

There was a long, ominous pause.

'What exactly does that mean?' Nicholas asked quietly.

The lightheaded gaiety was gone. The whole horror of the scene ahead dawned on her, in a flash. And she knew that no matter what, she was not going to do it. Not for him. Not for anyone. She couldn't expose herself to the camera, the crew . . . the vast anonymous audience.

'I won't do it!' she announced, clear and loud.

From the door, someone stifled a giggle. It sounded like Andrea.

'You won't do what?' Nick asked pleasantly.

'I won't take my clothes off. I don't care if you sack me, or blacklist me or sue me for breach of contract. I won't do it!'

'Who said anything about taking your—'

'Get Andrea to strip for you,' she continued, jumping off the bed, her arms still hugging her upper body. 'She's used to it!'

The room was deadly silent as she ran out.

Jo felt decidedly ill when she got to her sanctuary of her bedroom, and she barely reached the bathroom before she was violently sick. At last, weak and spent, her eyes streaming, she washed her face in cold water and then crawled into her bed, already terrified of the consequences of her rebellion. She just crawled in between the sheets, threw the covers over her head and lay in the suffocating darkness, wishing she were dead.

She knew it was Nick the moment she felt the bed rock under his weight. A hand crept under the blanket to find her tearful face.

'How are you doing in there?' he asked, politely. She mumbled something unintelligible and squirmed away from the invisible invading hand.

'Are you better? Answer me, Jo.'

Again she mumbled and nodded her head, still cowering under the blankets.

'Was that a nod for yes or a shake for no?'

'Yes,' she mumbled.

'I think you'd better come out of there,' he ordered, mildly exasperated. 'I can't talk to a lumpy blanket.'

Slowly she pushed the blankets away, and allowed her head to emerge and meet his cool blue gaze.

'All right, Jo. Now, what was that all about?'

Instead of an answer she repeated her declaration of independence: 'It won't do you any good, Nick. I won't do it—I'm sorry.'

'Won't do what? I honestly don't know what you're on about, honey.'

'Strip,' she explained patiently. 'I just won't do it.'

He said nothing for a moment, but his eyes never left her face. 'Where did you get the idea that I was going to ask you to strip?'

'What does it matter? You were going to, that's all there is to it.'

'Have you read the script?'

'You know I have.'

'Does it say anywhere that Melissa is required to undress?'

Jo hesitated, suddenly feeling uncertain. 'No, but then you often change the script . . . don't you?'

'Just answer my question. Where did you get the idea?'

She felt too spent to fight him. 'Andrea told me.'

'And was it Andrea who suggested you fortified your-self with half a pint of whisky?'

She turned her head away, refusing to admit it.

'Tell me something,' Nick suddenly switched the sub-ject, sounding as if they were conducting a polite social small talk. 'Have you ever seen any of my films?'

'What a stupid question!' she snapped. 'You know I have.'

'Ever seen a nude scene in any of them? I mean, real explicit nudity?'

She turned to gape at him. The blanket which she was holding against her chest fell from her limp hands. 'Well,' he prodded, 'have you?'

He allowed her a minute to swallow her own gullibil-ity. 'You might have trusted me a little, you know,' he said finally.

'It was a lie,' she managed to say, half in question.

'A practical joke, more likely. And a very old practi-cal joke at that. I should have prepared you for it. Especially with Darren around. He must have talked Andrea into it.'

'Oh, God,' she groaned out loud, struggling to free herself from the twisted bedclothes. 'I made a real fool of myself!'

She expected grim agreement, but instead he began to chuckle softly. 'I thought you said you'd never do it . . .'

'Do what?' she asked, puzzled, then gasped. While she was sick in the bathroom, she had loosened the drawstring which gathered the lose shift around her neck. The long, flowing gown, no longer held by the knotted string, simply slid off her body as she was struggling to squirm out of the sheets, and she was now standing in full view of Nick, with nothing on but her brief bikini pants.

'No, don't.' He was still sitting on the edge of the bed. His hand came up to arrest hers as she tried to snatch a sheet and cover her nudity. 'Just . . . just hold it.' It was one of his regular instructions on the set, yet his voice at this moment was not that of Nicholas Hayward, director. It was low, husky, intimately caressing.

Jo froze.

Slowly he let go of her arm and let his hand go to her breast, cupping it, hardly moving. His free hand began to move over her bare skin, the palm flat, fingers spread as if to capture as much space as it could grasp. Jo shut her eyes, willing all her senses to concentrate on that slow sensual voyage, as it moved across her flat stomach, her thighs, the small of her back, and finally rested on her other breast. Wherever it passed, it left a delicious limpid sensation, which kept lingering on long after the exploring warm hand moved on to new territories.

And then she felt her knees go weak as his mouth found its way to her bare midriff, the tip of his tongue retracing the inflamed path of his hands tasting, savouring every inch of virgin skin, guided by her own shivers to the more sensitive spots to pause and tease her senses to an unbearable delicious pleasure. When she no longer could tell which part of her was being touched, his mouth found her breast, and with a soft, shuddering sigh his lips parted to take it into a well of moist, sucking sweetness.

Moaning softly, Jo sank down on her knees, her body crying for something unattainable and yet so near, and nestled against him, wishing her bones could seep into his unyielding flesh. She struggled to free her head, her mouth hungry to find his, but his hand kept it trapped in an iron grip against his thumping heart. Shudders went through his body as he was trying to gulp air into his lungs.

'Nicky,' she whispered into the vibrant prison of his chest.

'Yes, honey?' Disturbed, she sensed him stiffen slightly.

'Nothing . . . just—Nicky.'

With a rueful but goodhumoured chuckle, he pushed her gently away from him. His wonderfully warm blue eyes were smiling. 'Tell you what, Joey. Whenever you want to cool my aroused passion, all you need to do is call me "Nicky", as you did just now . . . remember that for future reference.'

'Why?'

'It makes me feel I'm seducing a trusting, guileless under-aged nymphet.'

Jo twisted her head away, her cheeks on fire. Her nakedness suddenly seemed lewd, shameful. He couldn't be so cruel, so heartless as to tease her at this very moment about that miserable night in Corfu.

'No, no . . . you don't understand,' he laughed, drawing her back into his arms, not demanding and hungry as before, but cradling and tender. 'I adore it . . . but it does remind me that I'm responsible for your . . . well-being, shall we say?'

She pulled herself away from the security of his embrace. 'You mean you don't want me because you used to know me as a little girl?'

'Oh, no, that doesn't worry me any more. It used to . . . God, honey, I can't tell you how much!' Suddenly his eyes widened as understanding dawned on him. 'Hey, is that what's been bothering you all along? That night on the beach, in Corfu?' He didn't need a confirmation. 'Is that why you screamed at me the other night that I've killed the trusting child in you?'

She nodded.

'But didn't you understand? I had to keep you away, honey . . . and believe me, it was pretty hard on me. But after all, Joey, you were hardly sixteen, and I had practically been bringing you up . . . not to speak of my friendship with your mother . . .'

He stopped, as if once again the memory of Emma put an invisible barrier between them. She saw him fumble under the bedclothes, and finally fish out her crumpled, sorry-looking shift. 'Tell me,' he said as he was pulling it over her head, 'do you still believe in that nonsense about Emma and me?'

She wanted to tell him that she had forgotten all about it, so as not to spoil the truce of renewed affection between them, but she couldn't. 'Yes,' she said, her voice muffled by the folds of the garment. 'Yes, I do,' she repeated more clearly, standing once more fully covered in front of him.

'That's too bad,' he remarked lightly. 'But on the other hand, it'll keep you away from me . . . at least, until this bloody film is over. Now,' he gave her an indulgent smack on her rear, 'do you think you can face them again? The crew must be having a whale of time, imagining what the two of us have been up to for the past fifteen minutes!'

'Oh, damn,' Jo groaned. 'I forgot all about that.'

'Good thing I didn't, then. Come on, Joey. And don't tempt me again. Even with the best intentions in the world, there is a limit to my self-control.'

They were about to enter the crowded bedroom set when she suddenly remembered Lindsey's words earlier on that evening. 'Nick,' she stopped him, 'Why are you sending me away?'

'I am?' He sounded puzzled.

'Lindsey says you want me to go home.'

'Oh, yes, I forgot about that. I'll be working with Sir Daniel, mostly. So I won't be needing either you or Darren or Francis, for that matter.' Jo noticed that he hadn't included Andrea amongst the discarded. So Andrea was going to have him all to herself for a whole weekend.

'But why? Why send me away?'

'Oh, to hell with it, Jo! This is not a boarding school or a summer camp, for heaven's sake! You're not being expelled for bad behaviour. I simply think you deserve a rest and so do I . . .'

'A rest from me?'

'Yes, if you insist.' Nick groaned in exasperation when he saw her crestfallen expression. 'You seem to know very little about men, honey. Where the hell have you been cloistered?'

'I haven't been sleeping around, if that's what you mean,' she snapped. 'After what you said to me that night on the beach, I was damned careful to keep away from men . . .'

'Clever bastard, wasn't I?' he looked smug. 'Well, whatever you think. Emma has one thing to be thankful to me for. At least I saved her daughter from the hazards of contemporary promiscuity.'

She was tempted to strike him, but as she met his laughing eyes, she burst out laughing, feeling warm and secure in the renewed truce of friendship between them. She couldn't ever hope for his love, but at least the animosity was gone.

He didn't relent, though. Next day, Friday, after a full day's work, Jo was whisked off for a long weekend in London.

To her gratified surprise, Nick came out into the rain to see her safely deposited in Theodore Ianikis' luxurious Rolls-Royce. Neither he nor the producer would hear of her driving back in her Mini. It was raining heavily and accidents were accidents; one couldn't afford to lose an actress in the middle of shooting. They didn't seem to be very concerned about Darren, for he was allowed to go back in his own Ferrari—but then, he had finished his work in the film and was no longer their affair.

Jo noted, with a sinking heart, that Nick seemed to have regained his good humour. He hadn't looked so relaxed and cheerful in weeks. He was obviously relieved to get rid of her for a few days.

The sense of despondency was enforced by Andrea, who, for some reason, had decided to join the farewell committee, charmingly indifferent to the heavy rain which was soaking her hair and expensive clothes. Leaning forward to give Jo a perfunctory kiss on both cheeks in the usual film-folk custom, she sweetly wished her a good weekend, but the smile was hard and menacingly triumphant, leaving Jo vaguely disturbed and frightened.

The last image she had of Elmfield Manor was of Andrea, looking stunning under Nick's borrowed leather jacket, waving goodbye, and then slipping her arm into Nick's, to disappear with him inside the warm, dry haven of the hotel.

CHAPTER SEVEN

THE drowsy Hampstead street offered no welcome and the large Montague house looked aloof and gloomy, staring at Jo through blank windows as if doubting her right to be there. Even the act of turning the key in the lock seemed odd, like an act of invasion. Her home, during the last weeks, had been Elmfield Manor and her existence wholly dependent on the nearness and presence of Nicholas.

A dull pang of desolation shot through her at the prospect of passing four long days away from him. It was terrifying to think that for weeks now she had drawn all her energy, all her joys and sorrows solely from him. Irritable, rudely impatient, condescendingly amused, he was still there to colour the day for her and make life worth living. Again she wondered desolately whether he would ever ask her to work for him again. It seemed unlikely, judging by the obvious relief he had shown when packing her off to London a few hours ago.

With a sigh, she pushed the door open and walked into the house, which now seemed as impersonal and anonymous as a hotel.

'Who is it?' A whisper, hoarse and ugly, echoed through the silent house.

Her hand froze on the light switch and her terror escaped in a scream. She thought her knees would give under her.

'Is that you, Jo?' The croaking whisper came again,

125

sounding somewhat nearer but still unfamiliar and petrifying.

'Yes . . .' Jo's own voice was hardly more than a whisper. 'Who . . . who are you?'

There was a scuttle of bare feet on the pine staircase which led down from the upper bedrooms, and then a figure appeared on the landing, clad in a flowing white robe and looking in the dim light like a ghost.

'Oh, darling . . . you gave me such a fright!'

A second later, Jo found herself clinging to the tall, willowy form of her mother.

They stood there for a few moments, looking at each other, smiling foolishly, unable to speak.

'Mom . . . Mother, where . . . how—' At last the questions started tumbling out, in utter confusion; she gave up and simply hugged Emma again, just happy to have her mother back with her.

Half an hour later they were sitting in the kitchen, sipping hot chocolate from large steaming mugs and enjoying the old sense of companionship they had always shared. The long weeks of separation were forgotten now that her mother was home again, looking as beautiful and healthy as ever. Even half asleep and with her face clean of make-up, Emma Montague was striking. If it hadn't been for her thick, luxuriant silver hair, she could have easily passed for a woman of thirty. To Jo, she looked just as vivaciously young as she had always done. She hadn't changed at all.

Except for that strange hoarse whisper.

'What happened to your voice, Mom?' Jo broke into her mother's cheerful chatter. 'Have you caught cold or something?'

Emma said nothing for a moment. 'No . . . not exactly a cold, darling.'

The flood of questions gushed out now, uncurbed. 'Where have you been all this time? Why didn't you let me come and see you? You never phoned . . .'

'I couldn't, Jo. And I thought my letters would put your mind at rest.'

'Won't you tell me now, at least?' Emma remained silent. 'Can't you even say where you've been hiding all this time?' Jo urged.

'I'd rather not,' Emma answered, then smiled apologetically. 'Do you think you could trust me enough to accept a non-answer?'

This was an old way of avoiding Jo's childish questions. 'No, Mother,' Jo wasn't ready to play the game. 'I want an answer.'

Emma smiled. 'Well, love, I'm afraid I can't give you one.'

'Can't or won't?'

Her mother chuckled. It was an odd hoarse sound. 'Whichever.'

They remained silent for a long moment. At last Jo broke it with the question which had been tormenting her all this time. 'Weren't you disgusted when you heard I've accepted a part in Nicholas Hayward's film?'

Emma was plainly puzzled. 'Disgusted with you? What are you talking about, Joey? You couldn't have a better start than working for Nick.'

'Even after the way he had treated you?' She turned to face her mother.

'Oh, God!' the older woman groaned softly. A gleam of understanding replaced the puzzled look. 'So you still believe those ludicrous stories in the press? I told you to ignore them!'

'Don't you try that little game on me, Mother,' Jo said sharply.' I know what he'd done to you, and you're a fool to go on protecting him.' All her own unhappy frustration came gushing out, using her mother's as an excuse. 'He was ruthless, cruel and utterly obnoxious, treating you as he did. You were his friend and—'

'And he still is! The best friend I've ever had. If he were my own son, he couldn't have been more loyal and helpful, and . . .' Emma stopped, as if at a loss of words. 'He saved my life, Jo.'

The stricken look on Jo's face twisted Emma's heart. Her daughter, so serenely beautiful and seemingly so much in control over herself, suddenly looked lost and bewildered as she had remembered her years ago.

'I think I was wrong to try and keep you out of this, Jo,' she finally croaked, sitting up as if prodded by a sudden decision.

'Please, Mommy,' the girl reverted to her old childhood name, 'I must know!'

'Very well.' Emma's beautiful face hardened in an effort to regard her child as an equal worthy of her confidence. 'I'll tell you. But I'll start at the end: I'm all right now. It wasn't cancer . . .'

'Cancer!' The terror tore out of Jo's choked throat.

Emma's hand reached to touch her. 'As I said, love— it's not cancer. We suspected it was, but it turned out to be a tumour . . . a benevolent tumour, though God only knows what's so benevolent about it, except, I suppose, that if you compare it to the malignant variety it's quite appropriately termed.'

The story came out now, pouring out in that strenuous, hoarse whisper.

'I noticed the first signs—oh, at least two years ago, but I ignored them. It was foolish of me, because I probably could have saved my voice if I'd taken measures earlier. Anyway, just before I was due to start filming with Nick, I woke up one morning without any voice. I was dumb, Jo. Utterly, totally dumb. I had to be operated on without delay. They thought it was cancer of the throat.' The horrible word kept ringing in Jo's ears. 'It was Nick who took me to the hospital, stayed with me until the doctors assured him that they've managed to save my vocal cords and that it was just a benign tumour, and then he flew with me to Corfu, so that I could recuperate in his villa . . . protected from publicity and all those well-wishers who would have loved to know that Emma Montague was finished.'

'But . . .' Jo was still too numb to absorb the full extent of her unjust accusations of Nick, 'why didn't Nick say so? Why did he let the press accuse him of having sacked you? He could have just explained that you were ill and . . .'

'And can you imagine what would have happened to my career if anyone knew I'd undergone a throat operation? That I was a cancer suspect? Throat cancer?' Emma sighed impatiently when Jo still looked perplexed. 'Nobody . . . no producer or director would have been foolish enough to employ me again. I would have become a bad risk, darling, an unreliable investment. Even if I could convince them that I've been cured, who could vouch that I wouldn't loose my voice again in the middle of a fifty-million-dollar film?'

'You should have told me,' Jo kept repeating, once

she fully understood what her mother had been trying to tell her.

'Nick thought so too, but I hated the idea of worrying you. I knew you would insist on leaving the Academy and come to stay with me, and I didn't want that. Nick finally gave in. It was, incidentally, the only time he had given in to my wishes. I was quite ready to tell the press all about it, and take the consequences. But Nick wouldn't hear of it. He wouldn't even cast another actress in my role. "You'll be back soon enough. I can wait", he said.'

'Well, he didn't, did he?' Jo was trying to hold on to a vestige of her old resentment. 'He was quick enough to jump into a new film—'

'Oh, Joey, you really don't understand, do you?' Emma started to laugh, and even with that dreadful raspy croak, she sounded amused and lighthearted. 'It's the same film, my love. You're playing my role.'

'You mean you were . . . you are the mature Melissa, the one who recounts her early years in those flashbacks?'

'That's exactly who I am . . . now isn't it lucky that we look so alike?' Emma dragged Jo to the large gilded mirror in the hall and made her study the two reflections in it, one looking ethereal in a flowing nightgown, her silver hair cascading over her slim shoulders, the other, just as tall and slim and a strikingly similar if still unmarked face. They did look amazingly alike, except for the colour of their hair. Suddenly all those cryptic remarks about her resemblance to Emma made sense.

Finally Jo agreed to let go of Emma until the next morning. Her mother did look tired and drained by all the excitement.

'I still don't understand one thing, Mother,' she insisted, having tucked the older woman in bed. 'Everybody kept telling me that Nick was terribly reluctant to give me the part. Nick himself admitted it . . . So what made him change his mind?'

'Oh, didn't I explain?' Emma chuckled, delighted. 'To give me time to recuperate and still keep the press from finding out about me, I suggested he cast you in the role of young Melissa and got Michael Staller to rewrite the script and expand the role . . . In the original, young Melissa appeared in short fragments, as a faraway, misty dream. So you see, darling you really owe me a special thank-you. Because of my . . . my problem, your own role has been expanded greatly. At my expense, needless to say. And I assure you, love, I wouldn't let any other actress do that to me, except my own daughter!'

'So . . . so you talked Nick into using me?'

'Only after you convinced him that you were good enough, my love. Nick wouldn't compromise a film even for me. And it took some persuasion even then. He stubbornly refused to consider you, for a long time.' Emma's voice became thoughtful. 'I wonder why.'

Emma fell asleep before Jo was out of the room, but Jo wasn't as lucky; the joy at having her mother back home and knowing that she was healthy and well was overshadowed by waves of self-recriminations and shame at her own misguided distrust of Nick. She knew that she had been eager to latch on to the press's reports because of his rejection of her, and it added self-disgust to the already insufferable pain of being so hopelessly in love with him. And yet, now that he no longer regarded her indulgently as an irresponsible child, she had no idea how she could make him forgive her. She fell asleep at dawn, still smarting with angry shame at the accusations she kept throwing at him whenever her yearnings threatened to break through the hard shell of her resentment.

A sleepless, tormented night didn't prevent Jo from getting up before nine. She was brimming with energy and ideas. Emma had warned her that her return to London must be kept strictly secret. No one, especially not the press, was to know that she was no longer hiding. As a matter of fact, the only reason she had decided to come back was the knowledge that Jo would be tucked safely away in Elmfield Manor.

'They mustn't know I'm back as long as I keep croaking away like a lovelorn frog,' she explained. 'I must use the next few weeks for retraining my voice. If I ever manage to get it back, that is.' Her light, humorous tone hid a terrified doubt.

'But Nick . . . Surely you want Nick to know—'

'No!' Emma stopped her angrily. 'As far as he's concerned, I'm still taking it nice and easy in Corfu. So don't you dare tell him,' she added. 'He'd be furious . . . and I don't want to raise his hopes.'

Next they embarked on a fierce argument in which Jo, to her own amazement, discovered that she could be a worthy opponent of her mother's obstinate determination. Jo wanted to call Michael Staller and get him to come and work with Emma on her voice. 'He's trained hundreds of actors before becoming an agent,' she argued. 'And he, more than anyone else, has your interests at heart.'

'I don't want anyone here,' Emma kept insisting. 'I can manage by myself.'

'But Michael used to be a voice-production expert, Mom. I'm sure he can get you speaking normally again in no time. And I know he won't talk. He admires you—'

The older woman was still obstinately against it. 'Mother,' Jo said at last, 'I'm going to call him, whether you like it or not.'

She could see the astonishment on the older woman's face as she began to dial Michael's number. 'You have changed, haven't you, Jo?' Emma said softly. 'When I saw you three months ago, you were still such a nice, quiet—ever-so-polite little girl . . .'

Jo ignored her mother's inquisitive gaze. 'Michael?' she attacked the moment the phone came alive. 'It's me, Jo Montague . . .'

The agent didn't waste time on questions. The moment Jo explained the reason for her call he said simply that he would be there within an hour and hung up.

'He's coming, Mommy. And you're going to work your head off until you get your voice back . . .'

Emma wasn't listening. 'Let's have it, Jo. What's happened to you? Or rather, *who*'s happened to you?'

Jo pretended not to hear. She was noisily fiddling with the large professional recorder, preparing it for her mother's exercises and making sure her face was never fully exposed to her mother's perceptive eyes.

'I really don't need an answer,' the latter said finally. 'It's Nick, of course. You've fallen in love with him, haven't you?'

There was nothing in her voice to indicate whether she was distressed, delighted or surprised. The phone began ringing, and automatically, her hand went to pick it up, only to drop it immediately as if it were a red-hot brick. 'Oh, God, I almost forgot,' she croaked. 'Maybe we'd better take it off the hook. I might be caught unawares again and find myself croaking "Hello" to a reporter!'

Before she could finish the sentence, the phone started ringing again, shrilly. This time, Jo answered it, 'Hello,' she snapped, angry at the annoyance it caused her mother.

'Hello, lover!'

She didn't repress her exasperation as she identified Darren's hateful drawl.

'Oh, hello, Darren,' she spoke dryly. 'What do you want?'

'Obviously, I can't keep away from you, sweetheart.' Jo groaned. 'I'm so dreadfully bored!'

'Sorry about that, but there's not much I can do to help you.' Her eyes rolled up in response to Emma's silent enquiry.

'Oh, but you can . . . you can,' he chuckled, in his old seductive manner, already forgetful of her unambiguous rejection of his advances. 'Since I've been robbed of the joy of seeing you in Elmfield every morning, how about sharing my breakfast at Claridge's?'

'I've had mine already. Sorry.'

'I hate lunches, so how about drinks, at five, say?' he went on, before she could come up with an excuse.

'I can't, Darren. I have things to do and . . .'

'Oh, no, you don't, my love. I won't take no for an answer. Either you come here at five, or I'll come and get you.'

'No!' She could barely disguise her panic. 'Don't come here, Darren.'

'Hiding something, lover? Or someone, perhaps? I would have bet my life on Nick God Hayward, except that I know he's busy making it with Andrea in

Elmfield.' His seductive drawl was becoming ugly.

'I don't want you to come here,' she said simply, too disgusted to invent a polite lie. Emma, to add to her discomfort, was gesturing frantically.

'Well, lover, it's either one or the other.' He was plainly blackmailing her.

'Oh, very well,' she groaned, defeated. 'I'll be there, but I can't stay long.'

'Anything you say, my love. Five o'clock, then. And don't come wearing your jeans and the customary virginal white shirt either. They don't allow this sort of gear at Claridge's, you know.'

'Damn him!' Jo swore softly as she threw the receiver back on its cradle.

Michael Staller arrived just before lunch and Emma, in spite of her initial misgivings, seemed to relent. His dry, unemotional manner and his obvious professional expertise soon made her forget her fears. To Jo's delight, he managed to shut himself with Emma in the study, and after a few moments, the familiar voice-production sounds of humming, chanting and reciting began to flow out.

Seething with resentment, Jo put on a grey Calvin Klein dress which her mother had bought her last year in New York, pulled her hair away from her forehead with two shell combs and dabbed some make-up on her eyes, obeying the unwritten rules of Claridge's lounge. Darren was right. She couldn't show herself in one of showbiz London's favourite places wearing her old student gear. She wished, though, that he weren't the one to benefit from it. The last person on earth she wanted to dress up for was Darren Williams.

The gloomy splendour of the old-fashioned hotel received her with its usual haughty dignity. She had been there often, with her mother, and even with Nick, and always liked its air of pre-war pride in elegance and style. Emma had always considered it a most flattering background for her meetings with the press.

The thought of the press suddenly clouded Jo's mind with suspicion. There was something menacing about Darren's insistence on her meeting him at Claridge's. Scolding herself for having failed to fend him off, she walked into the cocktail lounge, and was immediately blinded by a chain of flashing cameras.

She found herself surrounded by a small group of reporters and photographers.

'Good of you to come, Miss Montague,' she heard a woman say briskly. 'We didn't expect you take time of your short rest to meet us. I write for the *Weekly Herald*.'

'What . . . what do you mean?' Jo gasped. 'I had no idea you were—'

'Of course you did, darling,' Darren materialised beside her, his cold, hostile eyes belying the adoring smile on his lips. 'She isn't used to giving interviews, you understand,' he added for the reporters' benefit. 'After all, this is her very first foray into the limelight.'

'Darren,' Jo hissed through her teeth as he pushed her into a deep armchair, 'I swear I'll pay you back one day!'

'Oh, I don't expect thanks, love,' he said loudly, wilfully interpreting her threat as an expression of gratitude. 'Why shouldn't I organise a little publicity for you, after all you've done for me!' He turned to direct his false worshipping smile at the reporters. 'She's been an angel . . . Nick Hayward is absolutely crazy about her.

He keeps telling me that he couldn't have wished for a more obedient, trusting, hard-working actress. Now don't deny it, love. You know he does.'

'How do you like playing Melissa, Miss Montague?' one of the reporters interrupted the actor's flow, plainly more interested in the girl.

Summoning all her self-control, Jo composed her features into a pleasant mask of polite interest and found herself answering questions, some trite, others intelligent. Most of the reporters were humorous, polite and flatteringly interested in her opinions and impressions. Only the *Weekly Herald* woman seemed bent on trapping her. It was no wonder. Her paper was one of the most vulgar gossipmongers in Fleet Street. It was the one that had published that poisonous item about Nick and Emma.

Jo was beginning to feel that Darren's malicious surprise party had failed to compromise her when the *Weekly Herald* woman threw the bomb.

'We understand that the part of Melissa was originally written for Emma Montague. How do you feel about stepping into your mother's shoes?' Jo gaped at the woman, at a loss for words. 'After all, Miss Montague, Nicholas Hayward obviously felt that you were the better actress for the part, otherwise he wouldn't have fired your mother and offered the part to you. But how do you yourself feel about it? I mean, isn't it a little callous of you?'

The silence was broken only by the clicks of the cameras, catching Jo's stunned expression.

'Oh, come on, love. It's an open secret, so you might as well answer them.'

She took a deep breath and spoke, her voice slightly

choked. 'I didn't take over. I'm playing only the part of Melissa in her youth. The important role, that of Melissa at the age of forty, is still going to be portrayed by . . .' her hand flew to her mouth. She couldn't tell them. Emma had made it quite clear to her that any mention of her returning to play in Melissa would be disastrous.

Desperately, she turned in silent pleading to Darren.

'She's overcome, the darling,' he drawled, barely trying to disguise his heavy sarcasm. 'The truth of the matter is that Nick is far too impressed by Jo, as an actress and as . . . shall we say, a woman? . . . to let her share the role with anyone. And we're all certain, having seen her in action, that she's just as capable of playing a mature woman as she is of playing a precocious fifteen-year-old sex kitten. Right, love?' He looked down at her, gloating. 'All it needs is a little make-up and a wig . . . and the genius of Nicholas Hayward.'

He was about to sit down, having delivered his message, when he added, as an afterthought: 'And by what I've seen on location, ladies and gentlemen, Nick is quite eager to give every moment of his time, on set and off it, to initiate Jo here into the secrets of our profession.'

'You . . . you snake!' Jo couldn't control her disgust any more. 'You're lying . . . you know you're lying!' She turned desperately to the reporters, who stared at her stonily. 'Please, you mustn't believe him. It's a joke . . . a sick, cruel joke on me! There's absolutely no truth about his insinuations—'

'Of course not, and we promise not to quote any of it. It's all off the record, isn't it?' the woman reporter grinned at her. 'Thank you so much for your co-operation, Miss Montague. You've been most illuminating. I hope we'll have more opportunities to meet you like this.'

'I'll never forgive you, Darren,' Jo said loud and clear as she followed the reporters out of the lounge.

'Oh, you'll be grateful to me one day, darling. We all need the publicity—and believe me, you're going to get it now . . . in buckets!' As she walked out into the street, two of the reporters were waiting for her.

'Don't worry, Miss Montague,' said one of them. 'We know a vicious set-up when we see it. There won't be any mention of your mother or your alleged relationships with Nicholas Hayward in any of our reports.'

Jo thanked them, weak with overflowing relief.

She didn't dare tell her mother about the disastrous interview. Emma was bound to blame herself for putting Jo in such a predicament and would have tried to repair the damage by calling the editors to tell them the truth. It would have totally ruined her chances of coming back without anyone being the wiser about her recent illness and the loss of her voice. Besides, Jo kept consoling herself, they had seen through Darren's vicious scheme. They had said so themselves.

The rest of the weekend passed quickly in the company of Emma. Michael Staller spent as much time as he could in the house, going only when he felt that Emma was overtiring herself, and his dry, acid but steadfast support kept both women from sinking into anxiety and doubts about the future.

When the production car came to collect Jo on Monday night, she asked Michael to see her out. 'Michael,' she turned to him hurriedly, 'what do you think? Is there any chance?'

Michael Staller always took his time answering questions, even the most trivial ones. 'Tell you what, Jo?' he said at last, giving her one of his very rare chuckles. 'Good thing Emma never fancied herself as a singer. Don't expect her to burst into a soprano aria, will you?'

'I won't. But how about acting again?'

'Well, I don't think she'll ever be able to project well enough to go back on stage, but I'm sure she'll regain that beautiful silky quality which I always admired in her. Don't worry, girl, she'll be back filming in no time at all.'

Jo looked at him intently. 'How long is that, Michael?'

'Two . . . three weeks. Don't ask for miracles, for heaven's sake.'

'Oh, Michael!' she breathed in heady relief, and leaned forward to kiss him. 'That *is* a miracle!'

CHAPTER EIGHT

It was only ten o'clock when the production car left Jo in the strangely deserted parking lot of Elmfield Manor. The giant generator truck crouched in its usual place, sole witness to any filming activity on the premises. No music, no shrieks of laughter drifted from the nearby crew cottages to break the eerie silence with the familiar sounds of an impromptu party. Jo could only deduce that they had all gone to Stratford for another excursion into the outside world.

The only familiar car in the parking lot was a white Porsche. She began shivering with anticipation and longing: Nick was there.

She didn't bother to stop by the reception desk in the hall. Her heart thumping painfully against her ribs, she was dashing up the stairs, gripped with a breathless need to see him again after four long days away. She knew he wouldn't be pleased to be disturbed in his private room, but she had to tell him she now knew the truth about Emma and apologise for her cruel, stupid accusations, even if her only reward should be one of his cool rebuffs.

'Miss Montague! Please . . .' The hotel manager came rushing after her before she reached the landing. 'I'm sorry I wasn't here when you came in.'

'That's quite all right,' she assured him, puzzled by his odd presumption that she was expecting him to greet her. 'Is anything wrong?'

'Oh, no . . . it's just that we've taken the liberty of moving you to another room . . .' Jo gaped at him. 'Well, you see, Miss Burton insisted on it and Mr Hayward suggested—' his well-bred voice dropped to a confidential whisper, 'I'm afraid Miss Burton was becoming a little . . . insistent, and in order to avoid unpleasant . . . scenes, Mr Hayward asked me to move your things to another room so that she could move into yours. I'm really terribly sorry about it. But it's a lovely room, Miss Montague, much nicer than your old one, with a view over the back gardens. It was Miss Burton's room, actually.'

'Obviously she has no objection to sharing a bathroom with Mr Hayward,' Jo muttered dryly. 'But don't worry, Mr Armitage. I really don't mind. Just tell me, where is my new room?'

'You're very considerate,' he praised her. 'I'm really most terribly sorry about this.'

Her elation sadly flattened, she stopped on the landing, undecided. Andrea hadn't been wasting her time, apparently. Jo's heart threatened to break as she imagined Nick and Andrea 'indulging' in each other's company, in the room which had been her haven for the past weeks: a secluded shelter where she could drop the mask of professional coolness and allow herself the doubtful luxury of wallowing in the pain of her love for Nick. Knowing that he was just a few feet away, beyond the accessible bathroom, did a lot to endear this specific bedroom to her, even if he did manage to avoid any chance encounters.

For a second she almost relinquished the idea of seeing him, but her need to see his face was stronger.

There was no answer when she knocked on his door.

She listened for a few seconds and then heard the faint sound of running water. Bracing herself, she knocked again, louder this time.

'Come on in.' Nick's voice was muffled.

Cautiously, Jo opened the door and looked in. The room was empty, but the bathroom door was open and the shower could be heard distinctly beyond it.

'I'll be right out. Don't go,' he shouted again. She could detect no sign of anger. He sounded cool and lazily relaxed as always. 'Who is it?'

Jo lost her nerve. In panic she tried to retreat and shut the door behind her, but the strap of her shoulder bag got entangled with the handle and she had to open the door again to free it. His voice came floating from the bathroom, no longer muffled by the gushing water. 'It's you, Jo, isn't it? You better answer or I'll come out as I am, which means my birthday suit, and chase you all the way to your new room.'

'Yes,' she whispered.

'I'm warning you!'

'Yes,' she raised her voice nervously.

'I thought so . . . Nobody else would use a mouse scratch to announce their existence,' he shouted triumphantly. 'Wait there, I'll be about a second.'

Reluctantly, Jo shut the door and searched frantically for a place to deposit her unsteady legs. The king-size modern bed, already turned down for the night, looked as harmless as a lion's lair. The only unsuggestive item on it was a crumpled newspaper, spread open to display the middle page.

A pair of huge, panic-stricken eyes glared at her unseeingly from a taut yet undeniably beautiful face. It took her a long moment before she could identify it as her own. Darren's sardonic smile loomed darkly in the background.

Even before she started to read, she knew what it was: The cruel vulgarity of the *Weekly Herald* woman columnist was unmistakable.

Clenching her shaking hands tightly behind her back, as if afraid they would be contaminated by a touch, Jo knelt beside the bed and leaned forward to read the framed caption under the photograph.

'Take note of this face. You're bound to see a lot of it. Her name is Josephine Montague and she is the star of Nicholas Hayward's current film, *Melissa*. And don't be misled by her youth or by that wide-eyed innocence. Josephine, or Jo as she's known to her friends, already shows a remarkable determination to make her way in films, even at the expense of her own mother, who is none other than Emma Montague. We understand that the title role of *Melissa* was originally intended for this great if somewhat mature star. But, to quote our reliable source, Nicholas Hayward must have had second thoughts when he saw the younger Montague version. And who can blame him? Twenty-year-old Jo is not at all intimidated by the rather daunting prospect of stepping into her mother's shoes. "With a wig and make-up, one can easily be transformed from a wilful young chit into a mature woman," we were told. Incidentally, Miss Montague Junior hastens to assure us that in spite of rumours and Nicholas Hayward's great interest in her, she and the international genius of the cinema are just good friends. Who are we to doubt her word?'

'So how about that, wide-eyed innocence?' Nick's voice was softly caressing as a panther's purr. 'Who taught you those subtle publicity tricks, Jo?'

He was towering above her, wearing a pair of old faded jeans which emphasised the athletic shape of the narrow hips and long, muscular legs. His upper body was bare, the crisp gold hair still glistening with water against the deeply-tanned skin, sheathing a network of rippling muscles.

Shaken as much by the naked flame his sight aroused in her as by the vicious words she had just read, Jo dropped her eyes to rest on his bare feet, which seemed the least disturbing item of his body.

'It couldn't have been Emma,' he went on speculating in a mildly intrigued manner. 'Your mother never had to resort to such seedy tricks to promote her career, not even when she was your age.'

'Oh, please, Nick,' she tried to stop him. 'It wasn't me—'

His voice changed slightly. 'Who was it, then? Your ghost? Your alter ego?'

She couldn't answer. Years ago, one of the girls in her boarding school had drawn some childishly rude symbols on the blackboard and managed to throw the blame on Jo. Unable to betray the identity of the real culprit, she had silently accepted the punishment. She felt just as hopelessly trapped now. 'Go on, then, let's hear it. Who offered the press this clever piece of filth?'

'It wasn't—' she tried to say.

'Oh, yes, it was filth . . . and filth is too nice a word for it too.' Nick's icy blue eyes narrowed suddenly, then roamed down to the spread-out paper on the bed to scan the photograph. 'Darren . . . was it Darren?' She didn't move. 'You got Darren to arrange a press meeting for you, right?'

He lost the lazy menacing coolness of the panther.

His hands shot out to grab her by the shoulders, clench-ed in an agonising iron grip, and pulled her roughly to her feet. His fury lashed at her in a cold, ugly whisper. 'How did you find out about, Emma? Very few people knew she was the intended star of *Melissa*, and I trust them all implicitly. So who told you? Was it Ianikis?'

Jo could only shake her head in dumb denial.

'Come to think of it, he did seem pretty smitten by you.' He let his gaze scan her body, coldly appraising. 'It couldn't have been too difficult to wheedle the facts out of him. I can see the scene . . . a middle-aged fool melting at the sight of your virginal aloofness. Did you wear your nicely starched shirt and tight jeans for him? Or did you try a new angle? Something slightly more provoking?'

'No,' she choked.

'Quite right too. White shirt and jeans are your best foil. Little girl blue, so sweet and unapproachable. No, you don't need to tell me—I know you wouldn't let him touch you. That's your greatest trick, isn't it? Do not touch, just look and covet. So the poor old bastard comes right out with it and tells you all about your mother's disappearing act . . .' Nick paused, his anger showing in short gasps for air. 'Well then, what's the next step? Corner me by establishing a fact via the press—is that it? Well, you're a fool, Jo. You know I don't give a damn about the press.'

'Ianikis never said a word,' the answer was forced out through tightly clenched teeth. 'And I never said any-thing to the press either. Emma made me promise not to . . .'

Nick interrupted her. 'Emma? Are you trying to tell me that it was Emma who told you about it?' She wasn't allowed to confirm this. 'You'd better think of a better one, Jo. Wild horses couldn't drag it out of your mother. I've been trying for weeks to talk her into confiding in you, and she refused. I can't say I blame her now. She probably knew how you would use it.' His hands released their grip on her shoulders, as if repulsed by their touch.

The incredible injustice of his accusation defeated her. 'It's no use,' she said tiredly. 'I'd better go.' She turned away from him, dragging her feet in the direction of the door.

'Oh, no, honey—not so fast!' He was there before her, wrenching her hand away from the handle. 'You're not going anywhere. You still haven't got what you came here for, have you?'

'What . . . what do you mean?'

'I thought the idea was to sneak into my room and make good your somewhat premature assumptions?'

Jo blinked up into his cruel smile: 'I don't understand . . .'

'Don't you now? Aren't you and I supposed to have something going between us?'

A warning bell began ringing in Jo's confused mind. The man who was throwing those hard, sharp accusations at her was a stranger she had met only once . . . that night in Corfu. But then she had been protected by her age, by her mother's nearness, by his old sense of responsibility. Now she was defenceless.

'Am I frightening you, Jo?' he asked silkily. 'Are you beginning to realise that you can't toy with me as you've been doing with Darren or with Peter? I resisted the temptation once, but I don't think I will again.' He leaned lazily against the door, his hands in his jeans pockets. 'You wanted to make a deal with me, didn't you? Very well, let's discuss it. You want to trade your ambitious little body against your mother's part in my film. Well, the answer is no. But I will take you up on your offer. Let's call it an overdue payment to the director of your first film. You must admit it's a cheap price to pay for such a golden opportunity.'

She had nothing to say to him. She was sickened by the ugly, coarse sarcasm. Once more she reached for the door-handle; immediately he slapped it away. 'Having second thoughts, honey?' He chuckled as he turned the key in the lock and threw it into the middle of the room. It was the violence of this gesture that betrayed the seething rage underneath that icy cold mockery. 'It's too late for that.'

'Nick,' Jo tried to steady her voice, 'you must let me explain. Please, please listen to me!'

The menacing purr was back, and very close to her ear, 'I will, honey . . . but later. Right now I feel like doing something quite different!'

With a shock, she felt the heat of his still damp bare skin burn through the thin fabric of her cotton shirt as he roughly drew her numb body to him. The furiously thumping heart and the shudders of repressed rage raised a curious flow of tenderness in her. She wanted to calm his tortured anger, to comfort and soothe him, as if it was he who was in need of understanding and support, not herself.

But this warm surge of love was instantly replaced by terror, real unimaginable terror. His lips descended on hers in one swift move; but not in a true kiss. Only to keep her open mouth from further protests. She choked as she felt the cruel invasion of his mouth. There was no desire or hunger in it, only insolent certainty of her physical inability to escape him.

She was held in helpless immobility by the iron grip of one hand as it imprisoned her head against his; only her arms were free to claw and hammer at his unyielding chest. His other hand, contemptuously ignoring its power to overwhelm her with the sensual intoxication of its touch, was pulling expertly at her shirt, then forced the buttons open and reached for the clasp of her bra. For a brief second he paused to savour the firm texture of her exposed breasts and then, as if indifferent to their allure, he dropped his hand to wrench open the zip of her jeans. Jo gasped as he released her lips and struggled to wrench the hard, careless fingers from her tortured body.

'All right, Jo,' he rasped in her ear, 'We'll take it very easy . . . very easy to begin with. We don't want to hurry up that slow-burning flame in that marble body of yours, do we? You need time, as I remember . . . and patience.'

'Please,' her voice was husky with fear. 'Please, don't!' She couldn't bring herself to call him by his name. This cruel, punishing stranger had nothing to do with Nick.

'Don't use that on me, Josephine,' he grinned. 'I'm not one of your little friends who need a touch of resistance to arouse them. You came here to get your pound of flesh, didn't you? To make sure that the luscious, mature part of Melissa was yours. So let's see how good you are at it. Show me how an innocent kitten can become a real, blazing woman.'

'Let me go!' she sobbed, and began to struggle, like a trapped animal, using her fists, her feet, even her teeth to free herself from those hateful arms, to avoid the menacing, glinting teeth which were trying to capture her mouth once more, knowing as she did so that it was hopeless. The contemptuous hands mocked her pitiful efforts and were skilfully discarding her clothes, pushing her jeans down her hips. Yet she kept fighting him even after he threw her on the bed and cruelly pinned her arms and legs under the weight of his own body.

Her sobs broke out dry and choking with shame at her degrading subjugation to his superior physical strength. Her naked back felt the unpleasantly dry texture of the newspaper beneath it.

'Oh, Nicky,' she called out, not to the man who was lying on top of her but to the one she had always turned to in moments of despair. 'Please come back, Nicky!'

She was free. Suddenly her body felt cold and exposed, but no longer violated by the stifling burden of his weight.

Her tears kept flowing out through tightly shut lids even as the stillness around her slowly seeped through the thick veil of terror. When she finally forced her eyes open, they encountered a cloudy blue gaze, staring down at her from great heights, opaque and unreadable.

Only the heaving chest and his perspiring face revealed the recent violence of his rage. An old T-shirt covered his upper body. Once again he was Nicholas Hayward, film director.

Weeping uncontrollably now, Jo rolled over to cover her nakedness and buried her face in the crumpled newspaper.

'It's all right, Jo,' he was gulping air into his lungs, but his voice was normal again, 'you're safe now.' He gave a hard, unamused bark of laughter. 'You remembered the magic word just in time, didn't you? Well, you won. Nicky is back!'

Her sobs were the only sound in the room for a long while.

Then the horrible newspaper was pulled gently from under her, and something soft and warm was thrown over her chilled body. She refused to look at him. 'I don't want you,' she whimpered into the bed. 'Not like that. I don't want you.'

'No, I know you don't. So don't worry, honey,' he chuckled softly, in unamused mockery. 'You're not going to have me.' The bed rocked slightly as he sat down beside her. She jerked away in fear, but he made no attempt to touch her. Gradually the painful sobs stopped tearing through her body, leaving it cold and numb and dreadfully alone.

'Come on, Jo. Put your clothes on.'

Gently, he tried to pull away the soft bathrobe which he had thrown over her, but she clung to it with all the force of her terror. 'Stop it, Jo,' he sighed, irritated. 'I said you were safe now.'

But as she still kept clutching the white terry-cloth material to her breasts, he took a deep breath, as if summoning reinforcement from a hidden bank of patience and tried again. 'Let's put things straight, Jo. I don't go for rape, never did, and you've known me long enough to trust me that much. Besides, anyone but an utter amateur in such matters would have realised that sex was the farthest thing from my mind . . . or,' he laughed dryly, 'from any other part of my anatomy!'

Jo just stared at him, unblinking.

'You had it coming, though. I had to get through to you somehow. Three years ago I would have taken you on my knees and given you the thrashing of your life. Today, I felt you needed something more effective. So you can relax now. Class is over. I hope you won't need a refresher course, and if you do, I won't be the one to give it to you.'

He stood up and walked towards the bathroom door. Her eyes followed him, but she refused to speak. 'I'll wait in there while you get dressed. Do you think you can manage now?'

She gave an odd childlike nod.

His eyes softened. 'Oh, hell, Jo, why did you have to change? You were such a sweet, trusting little thing once. What made you turn into a calculating, ruthless bitch?' He opened the door and with his back to her, he went on, his quiet voice expressing an uncontrollable surge of regret. 'If it was that night in Corfu, Jo, I'm sorry. Like tonight, it was done without malice. I had to protect both of us from your . . . potent charms.'

The moment the bathroom door shut behind him, Jo threw away the bathrobe and clumsily struggled to pull the tight jeans back on. The simple everyday task seemed as complicated as a mechanical operation in her awkward, trembling hands.

'May I come in now?' Nick asked patiently from behind the door.

'No!' she gasped, and started frantically crawling all over the bed, pulling at the crumpled bedcovers in search of her missing shirt. Then she froze.

'Oops!' a mock-apologetic gasp drifted in loud and clear. 'I had no idea you were here, darling.'

Swirling to face Andrea's amused voice, Jo let out a moan of relief, realising that the woman was not addressing her. She was speaking from behind the closed bathroom door. The 'darling' was intended for Nick.

'Do you mind, Andrea,' she heard Nick's dry voice. 'I was about to take a shower.'

'Oh, sorry, darling. Well, don't let me stop you. Go ahead.'

Painfully aware of her bare torso, Jo renewed her futile search for her shirt, almost sobbing in humiliation. She only managed to fish out her bra, its clasp broken as a result of her earlier struggle with Nick.

'Go away, Andrea,' Nick's voice was dangerously quiet. 'I've had enough for one day. Don't you start now!'

'Oh, poor love! Tell you what, darling, I have a bottle of Chivas here. Why not join me for a nightcap?'

'No, thanks. Just let me have my shower in peace.'

'You sound very odd, Nick,' Andrea murmured, her voice tight with sudden suspicion. 'And I don't believe you were going to take a shower . . . not in your jeans and T-shirt.'

'Is it really any of your business?'

The silence which followed his mild but plainly threatening answer shook Jo out of her momentary stupor. She grabbed the discarded bathrobe and wrapped it around her, then hurried to the hall door, abandoning her shirt, her bra, her shoulder bag in her need to escape the tale-telling untidiness of the bedroom.

The door was locked, and there was no sign of a key anywhere.

'You've got that Montague kid in there, haven't you?' The mellow tones were threatening to reach a well-remembered strident shriek. 'I know she's in your room, Nick.'

'Don't be a fool, Andrea,' Nick was still calm. 'She's the last person I'd want to see right now.'

A throaty chuckle welcomed his statement: 'I thought you wouldn't be so soft on her after that number in the *Herald*. The cheap little bitch . . .'

'That's enough, Andrea,' Nick tried to put an end to the interview. 'I don't think she'll ever do that again. She had to learn one way or another that vulgar publicity never did anyone any good. So did you, if I remember rightly.'

Andrea laughed maliciously. 'I, at least, was a little more subtle about it. Why, Darren says she practically let him put the words into her mouth! If they'd accused her of selling secrets to the enemy, she wouldn't have denied it.'

'What exactly do you mean,' asked Nick after a short pause, sounding casually interested, as if they were exchanging a juicy piece of gossip.

'I'm telling you. We had a whole crowd of reporters waiting for her at Claridge's and Darren managed to get her there . . . he says she fell for it hook, line and sinker.'

'"We"?' the word came out soft and light. 'You mean it was you and Darren who put her up to it?'

Andrea still suspected nothing. 'Why, yes. And she certainly gobbled it all up like a starved cat! Anything for a bit of publicity and a good part . . . All that good little girl and holier-than-thou act, while all the time she's been working on you to let her have Emma's role . . . her own mother too!'

'And where did you gather that bit of interesting information?'

'Everyone knows it. Why else did you sack Emma Montague?' Andrea replied sullenly. 'Anyway, it needed very little persuasion on our part. She was panting to pour out all that vulgar stuff to the press. We only provided her with the setting. I bet she'll learn to keep her mouth shut from now on. I taught that little minx a lesson she'll never forget!'

'Nor will I', Nick said quietly. 'I think you and I are going to have a little chat, Andrea.'

'Sure, darling.' The door-handle rattled.

'Not in there,' he said coldly. 'In your room.'

Something in his voice finally penetrated Andrea's smug egocentricity. She sounded frightened when she spoke again. 'She's in there, isn't she?'

'No!'

'I don't believe you, Nick.'

'She is not, I tell you!'

'Let me see for myself, then.' She was obviously trying to push past him.

For once, Nicholas Hayward's legendary cool seemed to totter. His exasperation and anger exploded in a loud, four-letter curse.

Andrea responded with a small, frightened gasp.

Jo no longer cared whether she found the key or not. A curious empty numbness replaced the terror and violent hatred which had been manipulating her frantic actions. In a curious daze, she sat heavily on the crumpled bed, no longer caring what happened next. It was all a dream, a nightmare, beyond her power to control.

She had no idea how long she sat there, rigid and numb. The minutes ticked away, in blank, grey monotony, and finally she sank down on the bed, drawing her knees up to her chin, her body clenched into a tight ball of shivering nerves.

She surfaced into semi-consciousness, feeling wonderfully content, her whole being responding to the gentle yet persistent stroke of a light, warm hand. 'Wake up, honey. I've got to get you back to your room.'

With a sleepy sigh, she nestled into a dark, hard yet giving mass of safety and warmth. But as she did so, she encountered the smooth warm skin of a human form, and she recoiled with a terrified whimper, pushing away the cradling arms.

'It's all right, Joey,' the same soft whisper breathed warmly into her frozen face. 'I'm not going to hurt you.' As she remained immobile with reawakened panic, he went on, 'I never meant to, honey. I only wanted to teach you a lesson you'd never forget. You needed it . . . I guess—' he hesitated, but then his voice hardened. 'I know Andrea talked you into that cheap stunt, but it still doesn't justify the eagerness with which you took her up on it.'

In a numb daze, she realised that nothing had changed. He still thought she had willingly given that interview to the press and tried to trap him into giving her Emma's role. Only now he blamed Andrea for putting the idea in her head. It no longer made any difference. She was beyond misery or pain. She jerked away as his hand came down to try and get the cover off her.

Sighing wearily, Nick got out of bed, leaving her shivering in the chill of her loneliness. 'Come on, you mustn't be found here in the morning.' As he switched on the bedside lamp, she saw that he was still wearing the jeans he had put on after their struggle.

The bright light penetrated her blurred senses, and she crawled from under the sheets, puzzled by the loose, soft T-shirt which covered her upper body. Suddenly fully awake, she pushed her hands under the sheet to reassure herself that she was still wearing her jeans.

'The key,' she remembered. 'I couldn't find the key!'

'I've got it. It rolled under the bed. Here . . .' he thrust something soft into her hand, 'your shirt. I'm afraid you won't be wearing it again, but you may keep my T-shirt as compensation.'

. He collected her torn shirt and shoulder bag, then silently let her out of the room and followed her down the long hall towards the landing.

They didn't speak until they reached her new bedroom on the second floor. He didn't ask for the number; plainly, he knew where it was. It had been his before he relinquished it to Andrea.

When he walked in after her, she made no attempt to stop him. She didn't want to renew any contact with him, not even the cold contact of dismissal. She just stood in the middle of the luxurious room, facing him stiff and coldly detached.

Now, protected by the impersonality of the untouched bedroom, Nick resumed his normal, quietly authoritative manner.

'You don't have to talk, Jo. Just listen, because this will be the last time we'll ever talk to each other as two individuals,' he said, leaning against the door, coolly staring at her expressionless face. 'By the end of this week I'll be through with you. I'm damn well going to make sure of it even if I have to keep you working sixteen hours a day. Once this miserable mess is over, I don't want to see you again.' He didn't pause for her reaction, his dry calm tone indicating that he knew what it would be. 'Don't worry, I won't do anything to harm your career. And besides, you won't be needing me any more. After *Melissa* you'll have them all panting to get you on their cast. You're good—damn you. Almost as good as Emma, even if you lack her character and professional integrity. But let me give you one final advice: don't pull that publicity stunt again. Film people appreciate ambition, but not vulgar callousness. Leave that sort of dirty fighting to hard, mediocre cats like Andrea. And incidentally, she won't bother you again. I told her to pack her things and leave in the morning. As for Darren, he finished shooting last week, but I'll see to it that he never repeats that kind of trick on anyone again. I'll never forgive him or Andrea for taking advantage of your greedy ambition.'

He opened the door and stepped out, throwing a final, cutting remark. 'And, Jo . . . try to remember how you felt with me tonight. I want you to think of me any time you're tempted to offer your body in exchange for a part. What I did to you tonight was only a foretaste of what you might be in for with someone who doesn't give a damn about your mother or about you. Goodnight.'.

The crew, unlike Nicholas Hayward, refused to believe the *Weekly Herald*; Peter and Francis made sure of that. Even Lindsey, jealous as she was of Peter's feelings for Jo, was too decent and sensible to use the interview as a justified cause for contempt or resentment.

'Only a fool would be taken in by it,' she said to Jo the next day, during lunch break. 'It simply smacks of a cheap revenge plot. I don't believe you said one word of it. Well, at least Andrea had what was coming to her. I'm glad Nick gave her the sack.'

She wasn't the only one. Andrea's dismissal was heartily welcomed by all. 'She'll sue, though. You can bet on that,' Francis warned Lindsey, since no one dared approach Nick with the subject.

'Oh, no, she won't. She'd be too terrified of crossing Nick's way again, if she wants to work in films again, that is. He's far too powerful and famous for someone like Andrea to tackle.'

'What about her scenes?'

'Eric is already rewriting them. Don't worry. Nobody's going to miss her.'

The fact that Andrea and Darren had been universally claimed to have been the main culprits in the affair made very little difference to Jo. Nothing could melt the hard knot of resigned despair which had been gelling in the pit of her stomach since the night before.

Oddly enough, she felt no anger or resentment. There was little doubt in her mind now that Nick's anger and contempt had blazed into such brutality only out of deep, unshakeable loyalty for her mother. She couldn't even blame him for being such an easy prey to Andrea's and Darren's scheme. She herself had been a victim of similar gullibility, urged by a natural if foolish need to anchor her repressed dejection. The only thing which puzzled her, mildly gnawing at the wall of her cold despair, was his rash eagerness to condemn her. She had never given him cause to suspect her of devious, callous motives. Even that night in Corfu, he had pounced so keenly and furiously on the assumption that she had been coldly scheming to tempt him.

The final days on the set of Elmfield Manor passed in a hazy blur of mad activity. The crew, pacified by the prospect of two fully paid weeks of complete rest, agreed to work every day late into the night. And Jo welcomed the unrelenting pace.

She was grateful to the crew and the cast for their gruff, unsentimental support on the set. For all their loyalty to their director, they refused to take their cue from him in Jo's case. So while he made no secret of his cold contempt, they kept encouraging her, dryly praising a particularly good performance or offered their seasoned critical advice.

'Don't let it upset you,' Peter whispered aside to her when Nicholas refrained, once again, from giving her any comments at the end of an intricate shot. 'You bet your life he'd pounce on you if he weren't satisfied!'

'I know, Peter,' she nodded.

'Still,' the cameraman remarked thoughtfully, 'he's behaving rather oddly. I've never known him to let his personal feelings interfere with his work. You must have touched a very sore spot, Jo.'

Fortunately, having worked with him so closely, she had become so sensitive to his moods and needs that she now could offer him instinctively whatever he needed to realise his vision of Melissa. In spite of their dead relationship, the bond of unspoken understanding persisted.

On the following Saturday, in the same mood of numb resignation, Jo packed her suitcases, thanked the crew, promised her special friends to keep in touch, and was finally allowed to leave Elmfield Manor for good.

CHAPTER NINE

Jo's homecoming passed in a state of dazed tranquillity. The quiet tree-lined street and the cosy serenity of her home offered a safe hiding-place where she could concentrate on weaving a new protective layer of detachment around her raw, wounded emotions. And Emma, instinctively aware of Jo's need for emotional withdrawal, kept her delight at her daughter's return in check.

She engulfed her with loving warmth and humour and carefully avoided any questions regarding Jo's last days on the set of *Melissa*. Only once, on Jo's first night at home, she broached the subject lightly:

'So it's over and done with, your part in the film?'

'I hope so,' Jo answered, cautiously. 'Unless Nick decides to re-shoot some of the scenes.'

'You aren't looking forward to that, I gather?' Emma whispered.

'No, I am not. To be quite frank about it, Mom, right now I don't want to set foot on a film set again.'

'Is that it, then? You're giving up your career?'

Jo thought about it for a moment. 'No . . . I still want to act. But I'd rather limit myself to the stage and TV. Films are . . .' she paused, trying to find the right words. 'I can't cope with the exposure. I'm an actress, not a freak.'

'I see,' Emma sighed. 'It's that interview in the *Herald*.' Jo affirmed with a slight nod. They had refrained from mentioning it all day. 'Well, as long as it's not Nick's treatment that decided you.' Jo looked up startled. 'I mean, he does tend to be a dictatorial slavedriver on set.'

'Oh, no,' Jo breathed in relief. For a moment she thought her mother knew something about her personal relationship with Nick. 'I loved working for him. He's a genius . . . and I don't mind hard work.'

'I'm sure you don't, love,' said Emma.

The two women looked at each other. Silently, the older one made it clear that she had suspected Jo's feelings for him all along.

'No,' Jo said firmly, 'it wasn't Nick. Though somehow I don't think he'd be sorry if I never made another film again, with him or with anyone else.'

Physically, Emma was fully recovered; she was bubbling again with her old inexhaustible energy and plainly impatient to get back to work. The quiet house was filled once again with the sound of the famous Montague "brown velvet" voice: warm, melodious and with that added touch of unique huskiness. Emma still used it cautiously as if afraid she'd wake up suddenly to find it gone again. But Michael was quietly confident.

'She could start working tomorrow, if necessary, but it would be better to take it easy for a few more days.'

'There won't be any problem about that,' Jo reassured him. 'Nicholas Hayward isn't expecting her for another week at least, and I'm sure he'd wait another month, if you asked him.'

There was another significant change in the Montague household. Michael Staller, silent and unemotional, had become a regular member. Even in her dazed, resigned frame of mind, Jo couldn't ignore the bond of trust and affection which was steadily drawing her mother and her loyal agent closer together.

The days passed quietly. Most of the time Jo was left on her own, as her mother kept working and practising with Michael. They only saw each other at mealtimes and in the evenings, when they sat contentedly in the small study, to chat or watch TV. In a way, with Michael there, it almost seemed as if they were back in the old days, when her father was still alive.

She never left the house and refused to see or speak to any outsider. She asked Madge to answer the telephone and just tell whoever it was that she was away. There were very few calls, anyway. None of her London friends knew she was back and the crew or the cast of *Melissa* were in no hurry to get in touch with her. They all needed a respite from each other's company after the claustrophobic closeness of a month's location filming.

But by the end of the first week, early Saturday morning, the idle telephone startled them all out of a deep sleep, ringing shrilly in exasperating persistence.

After six consecutive calls, Madge refused to answer any more, so Michael took over, and stationing himself strategically by the study phone, proceeded to pass the incoming messages to Jo in menacing patience.

'Someone called Peter. Can you return his call? It's urgent.' Or, 'That was Lindsey again. She must talk to you. She'll try again' . . . and, surprisingly, 'Darren Williams wants to take you out for lunch. I said you were out of town.'

Lindsey and Peter were the most persistent, but there were others, mostly members of the press, including the one woman whom Jo wasn't likely to forget easily. She wrote for the *Weekly Herald*. They all wanted to speak to Jo.

Finally, in a rare but impressive show of temper, Michael announced that he was going out to get some peace and quiet.

He was soon back, waving a newspaper menacingly at Jo.

'You'd better have a look at this,' he ordered her, throwing it on her lap. It was the *Weekly Herald*.

'I would never have suspected you of indulging in this type of literature,' Emma commented, a little dryly.

'Just read the middle spread,' he said, not bothering to deny the accusation.

The headline was almost as long as the item itself. Whoever had decided to print it made sure it could not be overlooked. It was an angry apology by the editor, admitting that last week's item concerning Miss Josephine Montague had been instigated by Miss Andrea Burton and manipulated by Mr Darren Williams, who openly admitted to his part in the set-up. 'I practically put the words in her mouth. Being unused to such old tricks, she was too stunned to deny or object . . . It was meant as a joke, of course, but I do see the unpleasant implications for both Jo Montague and her mother.' It went on to deny any insinuations about Jo's taking over Emma Montague's role in *Melissa*, and ended with a repeated apology to Josephine Montague for any distress caused to her. A smaller but very flattering photograph of Jo made sure the readers connected this item with last week's.

'What made Darren Williams confess?' asked Emma when they had finished reading. 'I know him, and he would never have acted out of remorse. He doesn't know the meaning of the word conscience.'

'My guess is that Andrea and Darren fell out and that was Andrea's little revenge. I can't see Andrea Burton meekly agreeing to carry the can all by herself,' Michael offered his analysis. 'What do you think, Jo?'

Jo dropped the paper on the settee. 'I don't know . . . does it really matter?' she said tiredly.

'Of course it does!' In her excitement, Emma's voice rang out loud and angry. 'I can't tell you how damaging that item was to your career, Josephine. I didn't want to add to your distress, but I was sickened by it . . . especially knowing that it was my own insistence on secrecy which kept you from denying the whole thing then and there.'

'Calm down, Emma!' Michael barked.

Emma obeyed without a murmur. Her voice dropped again to a guarded whisper. 'The only thing that kept me from coming right out with the facts was the knowledge that in two weeks they would be eating humble pie anyway.'

Jo remained flatly detached. There was only a slight lurch of nausea, a faint reminder of her initial reaction to the published interview. But the following events had paled its significance to such a degree that she could hardly understand her mother's present excitement.

It did explain the shrill activity of the telephone, though. When it started ringing again, interrupting their late breakfast for the fifth time, Jo turned to Michael.

'Are you expecting any calls?' There was no need to ask her mother; Emma was still adamant about keeping her whereabouts unknown.

'Not really.'

'Then would you mind if I took the phone off the hook?'

There were no objections. Jo stretched a hand to carry out her suggestion when the phone started ringing again. Automatically, she picked it up.

'Jo?' The sound-waves of the voice ran through her body like an electric current, making her head jerk in shock. The receiver dropped from her hand to swing like a ludicrous pendulum just an inch from the floor tiles. Nick could be heard, like an echoing loudspeaker, throughout the still room. 'Jo! I know you're there. Will you please talk to me?'

A silent sign from Emma made Michael pick up the phone. 'Yes?' he said pleasantly.

Jo recovered from her momentary-shock and calmly picked up her coffee cup, refusing to meet her mother's anxious eyes.

'He wants to talk to you, Jo. What shall I tell him?' Michael explained unnecessarily.

After a long pause, Jo looked up at Emma: 'Do you want to talk him, Mom?'

'No, not yet. I'm not that sure of myself.'

Jo turned to Michael, who was still holding the receiver, his hand cupping the mouthpiece. 'I'm sorry, Michael. Do you mind telling him I'm out? Or better still—' her voice rose suddenly, 'tell him I'm away. In Corfu. With my mother . . . Enjoying his lovely restful villa,' she ended savagely.

Michael delivered the message, verbatim, if in a less emotional manner. 'He hopes you're having a good rest,' he murmured when he hung up. 'And to tell Emma to take all the time in the world. He can wait. He seemed somewhat intrigued by my presence here. I told him I'm the new tenant,' and he gave one of his dry chuckles.

Calmly and systematically, Jo unhooked every one of the four telephones in the large house. When she came back, there was no mention of the last phone call. Only Emma's thoughtful eyes kept darting in Jo's direction as she was slowly finishing her breakfast.

The house relapsed into silence. Even Emma's endless chanting of voice-production routines was absent for a change. Madge had retired for a well-earned rest and Michael had a lunch engagement and, as always, warned Emma not to do a thing while he was away. Instead, she and Jo settled in the study to go over Emma's lines and discuss, once again, Jo's interpretation of the young Melissa.

'That was a short lunch,' Emma muttered when the doorbell rang barely an hour later. 'I wish Michael didn't retain such old-fashioned ideas about taking the house key. Oh, don't bother,' she stopped Jo, 'I'll get it.'

The doorbell rang again, impatiently. 'What's the matter with him?' Jo muttered softly, as her mother hurried out to the hall.

'I know you're there, Jo. So if you don't want me to raise the whole street, you'd better open that door!' Nick's voice mingled with the furious doorbell, then broke in an audible gasp. 'Emma! Good God, you're back!'

As if her body belonged to someone else, Jo noted in mild astonishment, that she could actually feel the blood draining from her face, moving in a sluggish imitation of its normal circulation.

'Nicky darling . . . this is a surprise! Come on in.' Emma's delighted laugh rang through the house.

'And you talk . . . you can really talk again!' Nick's usual cool voice rose in a loud, amazed pleasure. 'No one told me . . . I had no idea you were—Why didn't you get in touch?'

'Come in, Nick, for God's sake. I don't want the neighbours getting all curious. I'm not supposed to be back yet.'

The sound of the closing door brought Jo back to her senses. In a few steps, she was out of the study, taking the back stairs to her bedroom. Nick's excited voice followed her.

'And you're well? Really well? . . . You look great, Emma . . . and that voice of yours . . . God, honey, it's even more beautiful than I remember it!'

Emma's clear, husky laugh seemed to confirm his statement. 'So you think I'll do?'

'Lord, yes. Now I want to hear all about it . . . Are you well enough to work again? I don't want you unless you're absolutely, gloriously well again . . . what does your doctor say about it? Oh, honey, your voice! I really can't get over it . . . And incidentally,' he stopped suddenly, his voice dropping to a more normal pitch, 'where is Jo?'

There was a long pause.

'Where is she, Emma?' A growing note of panic replaced the earlier delight. 'She must be here . . . For God's sake, Emma, can't you say something? I'll never forgive myself if . . . I must see her, Emma!'

The anguished anxiety in his voice tore through Jo's numbed senses like a sharp raw knife.

Emma's compassion overcame her respect for Jo's wishes: 'She's here, Nick. But—I don't think she wants to see you.'

Nick remained silent for a long moment. 'I see.' Jo waited motionless on the landing, her feet refusing to take her to the secluded shelter of her room. 'Did she tell you anything about . . . about her and me?'

'No,' Emma said simply.

'You're not going to like it, Emma,' he sighed, 'but I have to tell you about it. You'll have to help me . . .'

Jo kept frozen vigil in her locked bedroom, numbly expecting him to come upstairs and coax her out. But she had nothing to fear. He left the house two hours later, refusing Emma's invitation for dinner and just going over the arrangements for her return to work.

'I don't want you anywhere near the studios before Wednesday, Emma. So promise me you'll have a good rest till then,' he said calmly at the door. 'And just tell Jo I'll ring her.'

'I know, I know . . . when you're through with the whole damn mess,' Emma chuckled. 'I've yet to see the day when Nicholas Hayward takes the time to deal with his personal life while in the middle of a film!'

There was no chuckling response from Nick.

'He asked me to tell you that he was sorry about . . . about the misunderstanding,' Emma remarked mildly later on that evening.

'That's all right,' Jo answered flatly. 'I don't hold it against him.'

Emma studied her daughter coolly. 'May I say one thing about it, Jo?' Jo remained silent. 'I can't excuse his behaviour. It was unforgivable . . . but, in a curious way, it was quid pro quo. You too have been accusing him of something which is utterly foreign to his nature. If you'd stopped to think sensibly for a minute, you would have rejected that stupid gossip item about his treatment of me as a ludicrous piece of nonsense. Well, Nick fell into the same trap. It is rather amazing, I admit. He's been long enough in the business to be immune to that sort of thing, but—' she threw Jo an odd look, 'You've obviously touched a very sore spot to trigger off such an unreasonable reaction.'

Vaguely, Jo remembered Peter using exactly the same words. 'I guess so,' she said finally. 'But I'd rather not discuss it any further, Mom.'

The subject was not broached again. But for once, Jo felt a slight pang of resentment at her mother's seemingly cool dismissal of the whole episode. She had somehow expected a more sympathetic, even indignant reaction. If she hadn't known her mother better, she would have accused her of egocentric involvement with her revived career to the exclusion of all other interests.

The news about Emma Montague was out on Monday. Ianikis, always a resourceful producer, didn't waste time once Nick told him about Emma's recovery; her name as the star of his film still promised a huge, inexpensive publicity. By Monday the press came out with a detailed if not altogether accurate report on Miss Montague's recent recovery from a bad case of pneumonia. A particular stress was laid on the star rejoining the cast of *Melissa*, as the mature version of the title role which she would share with her own daughter.

The Montague household reverted to its old, familiar routine. Once again, as in the pre-*Melissa* days, Jo was allowed to lead her withdrawn, reserved existence, hiding behind the fame and glowing personality of her mother. Her job now, as then, was to answer the phones, fend off greedy reporters, delay producers who were already brimming with plans for future films, and friends who simply wanted to express their delight at Emma's return.

Now that she no longer was in danger of being approached by Nick, either in anger or with polite apologies, she was quite happy to meet Peter and Lindsey again, but she never summoned the courage to visit the studio sets of *Melissa*, though she was very keen on watching Emma's masterful portrayal of her own part. The sight of Nick, even from a safe distance, was still too much for her still fragile immunity of despair.

Only once she felt her indignation rise above it; she had asked Michael, who was still acting as her agent, about possible work.

'I don't mind what it is, Michael. And I'll be quite happy to leave London . . . do a season in one of the reps. Even bit parts. As long as I work.'

Michael was curiously hesitant. 'Sorry, Jo, but you aren't free. You're still contracted to Hayward.'

'But he doesn't need me . . . I've finished all my scenes—'

'That's neither here nor there. Your contract stipulates that you cannot take any commitment until Hayward releases you.'

'Well, can't you ask him?'

'I have already. He won't.'

Jo groaned in frustration. 'But why? I can't be of any use to him just sitting at home doing nothing!'

'He might want to do some retakes. I can't answer for him, Jo. You'll just have to be patient.'

So she was forced to spend the next weeks in agonising idleness, relieved only by evenings in Emma's exhausted but happy company. When Lindsey phoned her three weeks later to tell her that Nick wanted her back for two more days, she couldn't ignore the slow current of excitement which seemed to break through her frozen feelings. She tried to tell herself that it was simply the prospect of going back to work, but she wasn't deceived.

'When?' she breathed into the telephone.

'Friday,' the assistant director was her usual efficient self, 'in Elmfield Manor again, I'm afraid. We're doing Melissa's wedding scene with you and Francis . . . The one Nick had cancelled.'

The script was still alive in her memory, word-perfect. 'Great! I always thought it was essential.'

'Well, apparently it is. There are too many references to it in the older Melissa's lines. The production minibus will pick you up Friday afternoon. We start shooting at . . .'

'Don't tell me,' Jo chuckled. 'Six-thirty make-up call, seven o'clock on set. Right?'

'Right. See you, sweetie!'

'I thought you were determined never to act in a film again,' Emma remarked dryly as she watched Jo packing a few things into an overnight bag. She herself was finally free. They had finished all her scenes two days ago.

'All right,' Jo looked sheepish. 'I've missed it, Mom. It's like a drug, isn't it?'

'What is? Film-making? Or making a film with Nick?'

It took Jo a second before she registered her mother's meaning. The stricken look on her face was answer enough.

'Come on, Jo,' Emma went on mercilessly. 'It's no use denying it . . . to me or to yourself. You love him. And you'll never be able to wipe that love or the pain it causes you by shielding yourself behind that passive, empty shell. You managed to do it once, but no more. You're not a child any more.'

The hard, sharp words pierced her mind like arrows, each echoing the deep, excruciating pain which she had been struggling so hard to suppress under a blanket of cold numbness.

'You must face it, love,' Emma's eyes spoke of her deeply-felt identification in her daughter's anguish. 'Otherwise you'll strangle the life within you. And don't delude yourself that you can live through your acting. A dead woman is a dead actress.'

'I know,' Jo whispered brokenly, and found herself held tightly in her mother's arms, sobbing all the pent-up yearnings and pain of the last few weeks. 'Oh, God, I know!'

'I know he terrified you out of your wits that night in his room—he's told me all about it. But I know you never really believed that he meant to hurt you. So be a big girl now, and tell him that he hasn't destroyed you . . .' Emma sighed softly, as she stroked Jo's dishevelled hair. 'Nick thinks he's done you irreparable damage that night . . . So will you go to him and assure him that you can still be happy and angry and sensible and illogical and excitable and serene like the normal, live woman that you are?'

'It won't make any difference to him, Mom,' Jo sobbed. 'He doesn't care about me. He liked me when I was a kid, but . . . something has changed him. I don't know what it was, but suddenly he stopped being a friend—and now . . .'

With her head buried in Emma's shoulder, she missed the smile on the older woman face. 'Just tell him you don't hate him, Jo. We'll think about the rest when you come back.'

CHAPTER TEN

THE main hall of Elmfield Manor greeted Jo with polite dignity. Physically, it hadn't changed much except for the marked absence of scattered lighting and camera equipment which a month ago had become an incongruous but integral part of the furnishing. The difference was apparent in the general air of rigid, somewhat stilted serenity.

Small groups of people in formal evening wear were sipping their after-dinner coffee and brandy in the small lounge which, during the filming of *Melissa*, had served as the cast's leisure quarters. Feeling a little lightheaded, Jo couldn't help giggling when she tried to imagine how these staid, respectable country people would have reacted to the rather outlandish humour and manners of her fellow-actors.

There wasn't one crew member, not a single familiar actor on the premises. She was beginning to think that in her initial excitement she had misheard Lindsey and got the wrong date; the fact that she had seen no familiar cars or vans in the parking area reinforced her suspicions. Then she smiled ruefully at her own doubts. The production mini-bus had brought her here. There couldn't possibly have been any mistake, then.

The lovely Chippendale table which served the exclusive hotel as a reception desk was unmanned, but she noticed a small old-fashioned bell on it. After a moment's hesitation, she went over and pushed it. A fresh-faced girl came hurrying from the office carefully swallowing the food in her mouth. Jo had never seen her before.

'I'm with the film crew,' Jo said tentatively.

'Film crew?' the receptionist said vaguely. 'How exciting! What was the name, please?'

'Melissa,' Jo answered, and then, seeing the puzzled look on the girl's face, realised that she had been asked for hers, not the film's name. 'I mean, Josephine Montague.'

'Of course . . . you're with Mr Hayward's party.' It was an odd way to refer to two dozen people who constituted a large film crew, but Jo refrained from commenting. 'Here we are—Room 6.'

It was her old room, the one that Andrea Burton had taken from her.

'If you wait here a second, Miss Montague, I'll get Tom to show you to your room, and help with your luggage.'

Jo smiled. The place had definitely been transformed. Under the film crew's occupation nobody had bothered with such polite considerations; people were too busy carrying out their own tasks to worry about others'. 'Don't bother,' she told the girl. 'I've had that room before and my luggage is really very light.' The girl threw a surprised glance at the small overnight bag. Elmfield Manor guests were obviously in the habit of arriving well equipped for a lengthy, elegant visit.

'Is there anyone else here? From the crew?' asked Jo.

The girl was beginning to throw bemused looks in her direction. 'What crew, Miss Montague?'

Jo tried again, patiently. 'I meant anyone of Mr Hayward's party?'

'Oh, yes. They all arrived an hour ago, but they've decided to dine in Stratford, I believe.' Jo declined an invitation to eat in the dining-room and opted for a light meal in her room. She now felt slightly petulant about her friends' desertion. The least they could have done was wait for her or leave a message, asking her to join them. She was starved of the sense of the old comradeship, the bubble of the communal meals, the noisy crowded drives to Stratford.

The moment she walked into her old, beautifully furnished bedroom, she was flooded by memories. To her amazement, though, few of them were painful. And Nick's role in them, overwhelming and memorable as it was, seemed surprisingly minor. Oddly enough, she realised, he had dominated her whole existence on the set, but was almost absent from her sanctuary. The only time he had invaded it was the day she had delivered that drunken proclamation of independence by refusing to be shot in the nude. Gazing down at the bed, she found herself reliving the enchanting sensual joy of his roaming hands on her bare skin.

Her mother was right, she thought. It was no use denying her love, suppressing her pain, wasting all her inner energy on forcing the lid down over her seething emotions. Once she gave in and allowed it all to rise again to the surface, she found that she could bear the agony of loss while, at the same time, find joy in the memory of those short but potent moments of happiness.

Still understandably suspicious of the strength and endurance of her new, fragile emotional maturity, she walked into the bathroom, breaking down one more barrier between herself and her memories of Nick. But there was little here to test her new strength. The sparkling ivory porcelain had been wiped clean of the past. Transparent plastic wraps protected the glasses on the sink shelves as a sign of unmolested sterility, and the numerous white towels felt cool and crisp and indifferent to her touch.

The door to Nick's old room was barred; from out-side.

Jo spent an hour in her bedroom, prolonging the delicious light meal which had been brought up to her by a young waiter she hadn't seen during her last stay. But at ten o'clock she gave up her initial idea of waiting up for Nick and the crew and decided to go to bed, feeling flat and rejected by their lack of eagerness to see her.

The sounds of approaching cars reached her just as she got undressed. Hurrying over to the window, she saw the mini-bus which had brought her earlier from London draw up outside the hotel, spilling a noisy, cheerful crowd which included Lindsey and Peter.

She was now seething in earnest. Why hadn't the mini-bus driver offer to take her to Stratford, since he was going there anyway? It almost seemed as if they were all avoiding her on purpose.

More cars were rolling in, in a convoy. She recognised Ianikis' Rolls-Royce, Francis Blakely's Morgan, and finally, Nick's white Porsche.

She didn't wait to see who came out. Excited, she pulled her discarded clothes back on and hurried to the bathroom to brush her long hair and wash her face, impatient to go down and meet them all again.

The next door room was coming alive with the sounds of its present occupants returning. Jo could hear the clink of the key in the door and then the murmur of indistinct voices.

Then, as she was about to stretch a blind hand for the towel rack, her face dripping water, she became aware of someone unbarring the bathroom door.

'Don't!' she called out, trying to warn the unsuspecting guest that he was bursting in on her. But she was too late. The door opened, and her heart leaped to her throat at the sight of Nick's tall, lean form, looking casually elegant in a black cashmere sweater and grey trousers which hugged the narrow hips and long, muscular legs. His strong, handsome face was drawn into a taut mask of shocked surprise, the deep bronze tan enhancing the gold shine of the thick hair and the deep glimmering blue of his eyes.

For once, she had the satisfaction of catching Nicholas Hayward off guard. He looked far more taken aback than she was. 'What the hell are you doing here?' he managed to say when he found his voice.

'Washing my face. It looks as if we're sharing a bathroom once more.'

Instead of a reply, he turned his back on her and called to someone in the next room, 'Whose clever idea was it? Yours, Lindsey?'

'What?' The American girl's head appeared behind him, looking more like a ten-year-old urchin than ever next to his tall frame. 'Oh, Jo, you mean?' And ignoring his angry stance, she rushed in to enfold Jo in a spontaneous hug. 'Hi there, sweetie. Sorry we weren't here to greet you, but Nick wanted to show your mo—'

'Do you mind?' Nick interrupted her before she could finish the word. 'My bathroom isn't the public lounge.' With new instinctive clarity, Jo realised that his gruff anger was hiding an utterly untypical embarrassment.

Lindsey was unperturbed by his dry anger. There was

a marked change in her usual deferential attitude to her director, as if she now saw him as an equal instead of 'the boss'. 'Come on out, Jo.' She was dragging Jo by the hand out of the bathroom and into Nick's room. 'Peter is dying to see you, and so is—'

Once again Nick stopped her. 'Leave it, Lindsey. Just go down to reception and get them to change my room. Why the hell did you put me here in the first place?'

'Why the hell not?' Lindsey retorted, while Jo almost choked on this cheerfully disrespectful defiance.

Nick was at a loss for an answer. The look he threw in Jo's direction revealed an ill-disguised uncertainty and painful concern.

It's me, Jo knew suddenly. He thinks I'm terrified of being next door to him again. She wanted to rush into his arms and reassure him that she didn't mind, that she wasn't afraid of him, and clear the look of naked pain from those blue eyes.

'I don't mind sharing the bathroom again, if that's what's bothering you,' she said instead. It was strange, after so many years, to feel again that uninhibited, trusting flow of love gushing out as it used to when she was a young adolescent.

'You're sure?' Nick sounded oddly vulnerable.

'Oh, yes. Really.'

'Well,' Lindsey broke in, having waited quietly while the subject was discussed, 'do I change it or not?'

'Oh, let it be,' Nick decided. 'It's only for one night, anyway.' Jo felt a pang of disappointment. She was looking forward to a longer stay. 'But do you mind leaving us now? We'll go over tomorrow's—' he hesitated for a moment as if uncertain of the exact term. 'We'll go over the arrangements tomorrow morning.'

'Right,' Lindsey saluted. 'Come down to the small lounge when you're through, Jo. We're all there. Nobody is going to go to bed tonight, I don't think. We're all far too excited!'

'About shooting one more scene?' Jo stared at her. 'What's so exciting about that?'

'Oh, nothing. I'm just bubbling, as usual.' And before Jo could question her again, Lindsey hurried out of the room, slamming the door after her.

For a long moment Jo and Nick remained standing, facing each other, awkwardly aware of the uneasy, heavy silence. There was little in the large room to remind either of them of their last meeting. Plainly, Nick hadn't even unpacked his case.

'I must talk to you,' he said, his voice tight and strained. 'But I don't think this room is—'

'We can go into mine, if you prefer,' she stopped him. It hurt her to see him so uncertain of himself.

'You . . . you're not—'

'Afraid? No, I'm not.' Only when she reached her own domain did it strike her that it didn't look too respectable with the crumpled bed and bits of clothing thrown here and there.

He shut the bathroom door carefully and leaned against it, his hands thrust in the pockets of his trousers. Jo swayed slightly with another wave of the sensual pleasure which his strong, lean form and chiselled face never failed to arouse. Not trusting her legs, she sat down on the edge of the bed.

'I . . . I also wanted to talk to you,' she tried to break the silence. 'I mean, there's quite a—'

'No,' he interrupted, 'you listen to me, Jo. I've got to say it. Not that it's going to change anything, but I must.'

The words struggled to come out of his tightly clenched teeth. 'I don't delude myself that anything I say will stop you hating me or—'

'But I don't hate you!' she rushed in, aching at the tortured look in his eyes. 'That's just it. I wanted to tell you that I never really believed you'd hurt me . . . and besides, I could never hate you. I—'

In a second, Nick was kneeling down in front of her, the gaunt, tight mask completely dropped, leaving his face naked and raw. 'I would give my life to wipe that night from your memory . . . to know that I haven't destroyed that vulnerable trusting innocence of yours.' His hands were gripping her arms, desperate to drill the urgency of his words into her flesh. 'You must—you must believe me, Jo. It doesn't have to be like that. It never is. Not with—with someone who loves you as deeply, as madly . . . as desperately as I do. Lovemaking can be so wonderful, honey. It could have been the most world-shattering, devastatingly beautiful thing between you and me, if only I hadn't been such a brutal, blind fool!'

Jo's eyes never left his, but she had stopped listening. Out of that tormented flow of confused words, only one single sentence reached her: 'Someone who loves you as deeply, as madly, as desperately as I do'. The words kept echoing in her mind, sending waves of irrepressible joy throughout her body. 'He loves me! He loves me!' she kept repeating silently, utterly deaf to his uninterrupted monologue.

'Please, honey, please don't shut yourself behind that impenetrable wall of your dead feelings. I'll never forgive myself if you do. You must let your emotions, your senses, your beautiful body come alive. Even if it's not me . . . even if you give it all to another man, I'll take that, if only you promise you'll try again—'

Her body, no longer governed by her drugged mind, was obeying its own needs as it slipped from the bed to the floor to kneel in front of Nick and sink into his hard, heaving chest with a groan of unleashed yearnings.

Nick stopped talking. His body froze into a still, unbreathing immobility. Only his furiously thumping heart gave evidence of life. Still acting mindlessly, Jo's arms clung to that lifeless form, trying to waken it with their own vibrant love, stroking, caressing, clawing.

And suddenly his hands came alive, gripping her face and forcing it away from the safe darkness of his broad chest to bring it level with his own. She let her eyes absorb the question in his troubled blue ones and heard him whisper her name in a husky low voice.

'Yes, oh, yes, Nicky,' she answered his unspoken question. 'I love you so much . . . so much!'

His lids came down over his intent blue gaze and his breath came out in a soft, shallow sigh.

'Do you, my love?'

She tried to nod, but his hands were holding her head in an iron grip. Instead, struggling against their force, she pushed forward until she found his numb, still uncomprehending lips and forced her lips onto the moist sweetness of his mouth.

For a moment, this was all she wanted.

But then his hands relaxed their tight grip on the sides of her face but still remained there, keeping her head close to his as his lips, tentative and soft, began their slow, almost timid exploration until, reassured by her evident hunger for him, their cautious quest was transformed into a devouring, demanding and at the same time selfless invasion.

As if afraid to blur the exquisite reunion of their starved lips, their taut bodies kept apart, refraining from any touch except for the light grip of his hands on her face. But as the kiss deepened, its urgency beginning to seep into their limbs, his hands, slow, unhurried, started to reacquaint themselves with the texture of her skin, the soft firmness of her breasts, the flat smoothness of her stomach.

Jo was sinking deeper and deeper into a mindless whirlpool of dark sensual abyss, incapable of distinguishing between her body, his hands, her mouth, his lips; her own hands found their way to the hard, smooth surface of his skin under the soft sweater, and her fingers, strangers to the wonderful silky texture, kept wandering with an excited sense of discovery over the rounded muscles, the crisp tufts of hair, following them down to his stomach and impatiently struggling to get beyond the restricting belt of his trousers. Her triumphant sigh mingled with Nick's tortured groan.

'Let go, Jo. For God's sake, stop it!'

She almost cried with frustration as his mouth tore itself away from her devouring lips. His voice, after the timeless dark silence of the kiss, sounded odd and distant. 'Why do you always have to push me away?' she moaned, almost sulking.

He gathered her into his arms, cradling her with controlled desire to his breast. 'I'm not pushing you away, honey. I never meant to. But have a heart!'

'Why? What have I done now?' she almost wept with bewildered disappointment.

'Hell, Jo, I can't take much more of that. I may be a repentant sinner, but I'm not made of stone!'

'But I want you, Nicky.'

'I know, my love. Thank God you do. I still find it hard to believe; I thought I'd buried you for ever in that impenetrable tomb of frozen senses.'

Jo tried to find his mouth again.

'Oh, no,' Nick withdrew his head. 'We've got to stop that, honey.'

'But why? Why can't I love you?'

He started to chuckle, and she felt her eyes fill with tears of overwhelming love. She had begun to think she would never again hear that wonderful, good-humoured, affectionate sound: 'Oh, darling, you can love me as much and as often as you can, and it'll never be enough for me. But not now . . . not tonight.'

He stood up, pulling his black sweater down, then bent to lift her deftly to her feet, his fingers already busy buttoning up her shirt. 'Everyone is waiting for us downstairs.'

'I should have known!' she groaned. 'It's the old Hayward motto again. Never indulge while in the middle of a film.'

'Well, not this time, my love. As a matter of fact, we finished filming two days ago.'

She was silent, absorbing the news.

'So what am I doing here?'

'I told you, Jo. I can't deal with my personal affairs when I'm shooting a film. So I gritted my teeth and bit my tongue and missed you like hell, but I had to get that bloody god-awful *Melissa* out of the way.'

Jo stared at him, still at sea. 'I don't understand, Nicky.'

He sat down on the bed and pulled her down beside him. Trustingly, not caring about any of it now that she knew that he loved her and wanted her to love him, she nestled into him and held on to his hand which she kept kissing lightly, endlessly. She only wanted him to stop talking so that she could drown again in his love, but his serious, almost solemn expression kept her in check.

'Do you remember what it was like when Robert died?'

She gaped at him. The last thing she expected was to be reminded of her dead father. 'Of course I do. I don't believe I've ever recovered from it.'

'I don't believe you ever did either, honey. That is . . . or rather, that was my problem, you see. You clung so fiercely to me after his death, you seemed so badly in need of someone to take his place . . . even at school, do you remember? You tried to pretend I was your father, coming to visit you, treat you to tea and lunch like the other girls' fathers. God knows, I felt rather foolish, not yet thirty and already burdened with a growing daughter, but I couldn't refuse you, could I? You were so lonely, so starved of family life . . .'

Jo was listening to him, slightly dazed, when in a flash, she understood what he was trying to tell her. 'Is that what you've been thinking all the time? That I was having an adolescent crush on a father-substitute?'

He nodded gravely.

'Good God, Nick . . . if that was so, I would have felt positively criminal, wanting you the way I did! I never thought of you as my father. I had a terrific crush on you when I was a kid. You were my hero and a handsome, a famous genius . . . but Nick, I—even then I loved you for yourself, never as a replacement for Dad . . .' She stopped, trying to find the right words. 'I love you as a man, and I want you as a man . . . I want to give you all I have and take all you want to give me . . . not stand by and whine for fatherly attention and care. Do you still doubt it? Or do I have to give you further proof of that?' She turned to him, eager to find his mouth again.

Nick started to laugh, an easy, deeply contented laugh. 'That's exactly what I wanted to know, my love. That's why I had to get away from you after our last summer in Greece. I had to give you time to grow up away from me, leave the choice in your own hands instead of taking advantage of a childhood attachment. Can you imagine how I felt, discovering myself head over heels in love with a kid I'd practically brought up myself, desperately yearning for a sixteen-year-old who was incredibly naïve and heart-wrenchingly trusting even for her age.'

'You loved me then? You didn't find me repulsive?'

'Repulsive? Oh, boy, Jo. You really are a baby, aren't you? I almost took you that night on the beach. God knows where I found the strength to reject you, and I won't begin to tell you how I felt seeing your poor, stricken face.'

'You thought I was playing a game, experimenting with you.'

'I almost believed it. I had to protect you and myself from your own innocent fire.' He pushed her gently away from him, his face tightening in memory of the years that followed. 'And I could not allow myself to take your love just because you'd been confusing me for years with the image of your father. I had to give you a chance to discover yourself, meet other men, test your reactions to strangers. And all along, Emma kept me up to date, unwittingly reassuring me that you are oddly detached, uninterested in young men, emotionally still dormant. She of course was concerned. I, to my shame, was damned pleased.'

'But when you picked me up for *Melissa*, I wasn't sixteen any more, yet you still treated me as if I were a—'

'I didn't pick you up for *Melissa*, honey. Your mother did. If it weren't for her, Jo, I would have never agreed to have you on my cast.'

'Why, Nick?' she asked quietly. 'I couldn't have been that bad. You said yourself that I was a good Melissa.'

'God, honey! How do you think I felt seeing that rat Darren touch you, paw you, kiss you . . . I was even jealous of Francis, poor devil, with his one pitiful love scene with you . . . Can't you see? I had to let them touch you, instruct them, tell them how to go about it . . . And to top it all, I had to stand there, sick to my stomach, and coax you into responding to their love-making when what I really wanted was to bash their faces in. Remember that bloody scene by the lake? Your seduction scene with Darren?' Jo nodded—as if she could ever forget it. 'I don't remember ever going through such torment. Forcing you into that freezing lake and then seeing you squirm in Darren's arms and having to bully you out of your shyness.'

'So you kissed me instead . . . to warm me up, turn me on for Darren.'

His anger blazed against her suddenly. 'Is that what you think it was, you idiot? Didn't you realise that I was totally lost, that I forgot where we were and what we were there for, like an amateur drama student . . . Damn it all, Jo, I've been waiting for that kiss for over three years! And then, after I had that one single taste of you, to be forced to keep my hands off so as not to jeopardise your reputation as a new actress, not to exploit your dependence on me as your director . . . and to see your bewildered, hurt eyes and be unable to comfort and reassure you. It was pure hell, my love.'

'I still don't see why you had to keep away,' she said.

'I wanted to love you as a woman, Jo, not as a trusting child, or a sexually aroused adolescent. If only you'd told me on our first night here, remember? When we met in the bathroom . . . if only you'd told me then that you didn't believe those lousy reports in the press . . . You threw your hate in my face with such convincing vehemence.' He groaned. 'God, I wish you'd told me then that you loved me!'

'I wish you'd told me how you felt about me when we were in Corfu instead of walking out of my life,' she retorted.

'I wish I'd come back before we got involved with shooting *Melissa*—'

'I wish . . .' Jo stopped and started to giggle. 'Oh, Nick, I wish you'd stop talking and make love to me!'

He paused for a moment, then grinned:

'Not tonight, Josephine.'

After a stunned silence, they both shrieked with laughter. Finally, her eyes still streaming with tears, Jo managed to breathe: 'Why not? The film is over, I'm almost twenty-one, and you can't suspect me any more of hating you or of loving you like a father . . . So, Mr Hayward, why not tonight?'

'Well,' he said lazily, his fingers tracing a loving path along her cheeks, across her lips, dropping to stroke her long, graceful neck, 'there's this little matter of getting married.'

'Married?' she gaped at him. 'Who's talking about marriage?'

'I am . . . and so are you. That's what we're here for.'

'Marriage? I thought you'd brought me over to shoot a few more scenes!'

Nick looked a little sheepish and smugly pleased with himself. 'Well, I'm afraid I got you here under false pretences. The truth is that I've got them all here for our wedding. Your mother and Madge, Lindsey, Peter and Eric and Ianikis . . . the whole bloody crew, in fact. Even that lanky agent of yours, what's-his-name Staller . . .'

'What . . . what are you talking about?'

'The wedding, my love. We're getting married tomorrow, if you'll have me, that is.'

'You mean you've organised our wedding here? In Elmfield Manor?'

'Yes.'

'But earlier on . . . you thought I hated you . . . You twisted my heart, looking so worried and unsure . . . Was it all an act?'

Nick groaned, remembering. 'I wish it were, Jo. But no. I went through hell, darling. I wasn't sure of you at all. But Emma . . . it was her idea. She thought I wouldn't have any trouble convincing you that we're doomed to spend the rest of our lives together. What are you doing?'

His puzzled question came as Jo, calm and firm, stood up, went to the bathroom door, locked it and then proceeded to do the same with the hall door, then with one smooth gesture she threw both keys out of the open Georgian windows.

'You idiot!' Nick gaped at her, resuming once again

his old exasperated, impatient director's manner. 'What the hell made you do such a crazy, stupid . . .'

Still calm and determined, Jo returned to the bed and smiled at his furious face. 'For once, Nicholas Hayward, for once I'm going to call the shots. You're staying here tonight, or else!'

'Or else?' Slowly the angry scowl faded away and his deep blue eyes began to sparkle dangerously.

'Or else, no wedding tomorrow. All the best-laid plans of mice and men gone down the drain. Nicholas Hayward would never be able to face the world again.'

'Oh, well,' he threw himself on the bed, spreading his arms across its vast expanse, 'I know when I'm licked. But don't think I'm going to surrender unconditionally.'

'Oh, yeah?' Jo looked down at him haughtily. 'What are your terms, then?'

'You never make another film!'

'Not even with you?'

'Especially not with me!'

She let him wait a long moment before she gave her answer. 'Well, come on, honey,' he urged, wavering between smug confidence and anxious uncertainty. 'Is it a deal or not?'

'Oh, all right,' she conceded graciously. 'No more film-making. I'll settle for the film-maker instead.'

Slowly, no longer laughing, she lowered herself to meet his open, hungry arms and let his strong, overflowing love drown her in a timeless, endless bliss.

Coming Next Month in Harlequin Romance!

2635 A FIERCE ENCOUNTER Jane Donnelly
The reappearance of an old flame after five long years throws a young Midlands girl for a loop. Worse still to have to act opposite him in a romantic play that parallels their own love!

2636 THE STREET OF THE FOUNTAIN Madeleine Ker
Exotic Instanbul forms the exciting backdrop for this intrigue-laden love story of two archeologists — one a lovely "English rose" and the other a handsome and mysterious Hungarian.

2637 THE ROAD TO FOREVER Jeneth Murrey
Life can be just as complicated in a quiet Welsh village as it is in bustling London. So discovers Lallie Moncke when she poses as the fiancée of a disturbing Welshman from her past.

2638 STARFIRE Celia Scott
A Canadian film director and a beautiful English actress cross swords while filming on location in Quebec. Their animosity changes to tempestuous love — which the fates seem determined to impede!

2639 NO ALTERNATIVE Margaret Way
When the alternatives are remarry a ruthless ex-husband or allow a ne'er-do-well brother to go to jail, a pretty Australian secretary chooses the former, despite her grave misgivings....

2640 THE TYZAK INHERITANCE Nicola West
The joint managing directors — one an heiress, the other an artistic Welshman — of an English fine-crystal manufacturing firm don't see eye to eye when it comes to business — or love!